Theaker's Quarterly Fiction #58

Edited by
Douglas J. Ogurek

Theaker's Quarterly Fiction #58

Edited by Douglas J. Ogurek

Cover Artist

Howard Watts

Contributors

Antonella Coriander
Drew Tapley
Howard Watts
M.S. Swift
Rafe McGregor
Rose M. Rye
Stephen Theaker

Contents

Editorial

Fiction

The Quarterly Review

6　　CONTENTS

Virtue in the Muck: the Making of a Subgenre

Douglas J. Ogurek

A death metal song drew me in. It was powerful, melodic, and enchantingly dark. Far too extreme and controversial for the average person... something that an introverted guy like me would really like. Then I discovered the video, a surreal and somewhat diabolical affair. I watched it daily. Symphonic black metal, they call the subgenre. It combines the brutality of death metal with the beauty of symphonic and orchestral music. Singing joins growling, synthesizers merge with guitars. Imagine *The Texas Chainsaw* massacre with a Lord of the Rings or Harry Potter soundtrack.

Then I introduced the song to my wife, another death metal fan. She watched the video without comment, and when it ended, she reflected a bit before giving her assessment: "That might be the best song I've ever heard." Then she said, "We can never listen to it again." Her comment refers to the song's lyrical content, which blatantly attacks our belief system.

Though I did stop listening to that song, I craved another dose of its dark beauty. Fortunately, I discovered another subgenre called "unblack metal".

Musically, it offered the same feel as the song that we banned from our ears. Even the vocalists, whose delivery ranged from Gollumesque to something like a T-rex, belted out similarly *sounding* unintelligible lyrics. However, a quick google search of those unblack metal lyrics offers a pleasant surprise: a positive message. In some cases, it's a direct admission of faith. In others, it's a quiet or cryptic nod to humanitarianism.

So I asked myself: how can I, as a writer, apply this vile container/altruistic contents concept to literature? The answer came to me like a mallet to the cranium: splatterpunk, horror's most controversial subgenre. These tales of sexual deviation and over-the-top violence committed by eccentric and often depraved individuals aim to gross out followers and offend dissenters. This isn't the stuff you'll find in high school syllabi, nor is it in the "recommended reads" section of your local library. Heck, it's probably not even in your library.

What if, like unblack metal, these extreme horror stories could offer a positive message, whether blatant or subtle, within their otherwise vile contents? Thus was born unsplatterpunk.

I'm elated to introduce a group of talented and open-minded writers in this first ever anthology of unsplatterpunk stories. This isn't a volume you'd want to pull out on family reading night, and you might want to avoid discussing it in detail with your coworkers. But it *is* interesting, damn it!

In M.S. Swift's deliberately disjointed "A Desert of Shadow and Bone", brutality meets philosophy in an extravaganza of limb hacking, gentry slaughtering, and drug use that makes a statement about corporate greed and the repression of women. What starts as an extreme, albeit intimate ritual beside a tree-lined natural pool builds to a climax that is both apocalyptic and indicative of personal growth.

There's something awry about an impending birth in "Quand les queues s'allongèrent". When you discover what it is, you'll get a jolt of humour and revulsion. Antonella Coriander offers a slashing take on misogyny and women's empowerment.

Drew Tapley's "The Fisherman's Ring" delves into the absurd as he unveils what really happens in the secretive ceremony to select the next Pope. You get ringside seats for a series of trials full of pain-tertainment. You also get hope and solidarity.

In "The Armageddon Coat", the collection's longest work, Howard Watts takes us on a more serious journey of two pre-teens as they try to make sense of their world following an alien attack. The theme of innocence vs. experience swirls amid political maneuvering, mass destruction, and vicious fighting to survive.

Though these stories vary greatly in style and subject matter, they all offer a measure of virtue within the muck. They may offend many, but the hope is that they will entertain and perhaps even embolden a few to embrace more benevolent behaviours.

I extend a special thanks to Stephen Theaker for his devotion to genre fiction and enthusiastic support of emerging artists, and to Howard Watts for this volume's in-your-face cover art. There is nothing remotely friendly or welcoming about that cadaverous visage. In a way, Watts's alien throws out a challenge to the reader: the contents of this collection may pull you away from humanity, but perhaps when you least expect, they'll bring you right back. Are you ready?

Just like the punky protagonists in M.S. Swift's story get sucked into a sick ritual, we get drawn to the violence that fills our world. We can't escape it, but maybe we can use it to make the world better.

When it comes to faith and purpose, everyone who encounters this volume likely envisions a different way to overcome the obstacles that life throws at us. With the unsplatterpunk subgenre, however, maybe there is one way that we can agree upon: over the top.

Douglas J. Ogurek

PAY £5 TO COMIC RELIEF AND TQF WILL REVIEW YOUR BOOK. (BUT WE WON'T READ IT.)

Fundraising for Red Nose Day

#rednosereviews

This March, for one day only, Stephen will be setting aside his scruples, taking your filthy backhanders, and giving glowing reviews to books he's never read, all in aid of Comic Relief. This is a great way to publicise your book while supporting a good cause. We are taking bookings in advance. The link below will take you to our Red Nose Day page. Make a donation of five pounds per book, and then email us with the cover and blurb. The reviews will be written and published to the TQF blog on Red Nose Day (Friday, 24 March 2017) in the order in which they are booked, and will also appear in a subsequent issue of the magazine.

www.justgiving.com/fundraising/ corruptreviewsforcash

A Desert of Shadow and Bone

M.S. Swift

The old man levelled his shotgun at me. When he spoke it was in the clipped tones of the moneyed classes.

"The only woman who should be wielding a blade, young lady, is an assistant to a chef. I am more than happy to add more metal to that face of yours!"

"Lori." Tor didn't break his stride. His remaining hand swung back the sword ready for a slash to the head. The gun cracked. It knocked over the old man and the shot flung Tor back onto the lawn.

Behind the ornate patio doors, some guests stared in shock, others beckoned the old man inside, and a few celebrated the lucky shot.

The old man, now risen, fumbled the reload, then fled back into the house through the kitchen door.

Tor was sprawled beyond the reach of the security lights. None within had witnessed his left shoulder blow out; they all thought he was dead.

Arna tucked stray dreadlocks back into her ponytail as she and I watched Tor leap back to his feet. With his arm dangling from a mesh of sinew, he stealthily headed toward the house. Screams from the pool area made an appropriate soundtrack to his approach. When he reached the mansion and threw himself headfirst through an open utility window, breathless anticipation gave way to burning conviction once again. A moment passed before his bloodied form burst into the well-lit living room. We watched its inhabitants whirl and scream as the sword swept through them.

Moments later, blood curtained the patio doors. Arna and I approached the kitchen door with axe, bottle, and scalpel ready to meet the rush...

Victor (Tor to his friends) and I had arrived at the party intending to serve drinks rather than massacre everyone. Six weeks had passed since I had broken up with him. It had been a long time coming, but the final straw was when he'd returned drunk to our squat in the disused school on the edge of town. He was playing up to a couple of friends when he laughed at me for flicking through a tarot pack. He ranted that there was no destiny in life, that fantasy worlds "disguised the brutal repression of a post-Brexit, neoliberal Tory hell" and claimed that he would never sell out and "work for those rich cunts as a fucking fortune teller!" I hadn't believed the cards could tell anyone's fortune, but I liked the images; they were drawn in a Celtic style and depicted a world of wise-eyed lords and elfin ladies who all emitted a strange, inner light.

Despite all of this, Tor and I remained on speaking terms and helped each other out with cider and drugs. Then Jaxi, a fellow squatter, offered me two positions waiting at an exclusive house party after she and her boyfriend had committed elsewhere. I knew that Tor needed the money, so I accepted for both of us.

We had taken a late afternoon train to the end of the line where the urban concrete made way for the fields and woods of West Wirral. We walked down the stretch of country lane through spring fields that seemed a world away from the wastelands of Merseyside. It felt good to be out of the city now that May had arrived, especially since Tor had brought a couple of bottles of strong cider with him to make the walk more palatable. We were responsible drunk walkers: we took our empties with us and I made sure he shielded me when I pissed in the hedgerow.

After walking for an hour and a half, we found the address, a palatial new build with landscaped grounds overlooking the Dee Estuary. Unfortunately for the guests, the bouncers at the gate wouldn't let us in. They were the sort who stuck England flags outside their houses and they did the usual routine of questioning our gender, sexuality, and housing status. When we confirmed that we were of no fixed abode, they became heated and tried to pull the piercings out of our faces. At that point, a well-dressed older lady had approached from the garden. She wrinkled up her face and made some comment about us crawling out from under stones, then ordered her henchmen to drive us away. I wasn't entirely surprised. Although we had made an effort for this job – I had on a black, long-sleeved top and Tor had turned his Discharge T-shirt inside out – I had been a little sick on the way and we had both licked a droplet of liquid acid from the jar I kept in my bag.

My parting comments earned us an angry pursuit, which was only given up after we cut across a field, threw ourselves over a barbed wire fence, and then scrabbled down into a sandstone gulley.

One of those middle-aged rich women was first. I waited behind the kitchen door and when she emerged, I seized a handful of her layered, tinted hair, pulled it taut, and then ground a shattered bottle into her face. I felt her skin puncture and an eye pop. When she bit down on the glass, I jabbed it deeper so that it raked the roof of her mouth and the back of her throat. The pierced eye was running down her nose like a huge snot trail when I smashed her head into a man's wild-eyed face that appeared from the kitchen door.

Arna had axed a couple of others and several more tumbled over those bodies to land at our feet. Those behind diverted back for another escape route. Screams from within reassured me that Tor's injury did not hinder him. As I opened up the skin before me, I reflected on how easy drunken people were to kill when an unworldly fire spits and hungers and seethes within one's core.

Once Tor and I made it over the fence, the bouncers gave up. Their final bellowed insults seemed a world away from the sunken copse of trees growing from the sodden ground beneath us. Exhausted, we slid down a tree and sat at its roots. Crows perched silently in the canopy above us.

We talked about the injustice of it all. We lived in an urban shithole where we couldn't even afford a room. And those who did have work lived in houses crammed with two or three families. Out here, with all the space and the light, the landlords, loan sharks, estate agents, and bosses of security firms lived in luxury.

The acid must have started kicking in at that point: I glimpsed a white shape. It flickered just beyond the largest tree whose lower branches extended over a broad pool. The tree obstructed my view, but I was certain that something shifted from side to side over the water like a giant arm waving from the depths. I left Tor fumbling over a spliff and picked my way toward the pool. A huge arch of what could have been bone rose from the middle of the dark water. It kept shifting, and seemed to be pulsing and shivering. I decided that it was the trunk of a partly-submerged tree rather than a massive, living bone. I giggled at that idea.

Hearing Tor talking to himself, I ducked under low-reaching leaves when something dragged against my shoulder and I was tapped on the head. Suspended from the branches were small parcels bound in weather-stained fabric and tied with wire or ribbon.

The way that the breeze hit the leaves created the impression of whispering (or hissing) above me. Something flitted across my vision. A fox stared at me. It had a thin, pale object in its mouth. It scurried into the undergrowth beyond the big tree leaving me sure that the object it had clamped in its jaws was a bone.

That was the point when I noticed that the hangings were concentrated around the water closest to the dead tree, and that shards of bone protruded from the gently swaying fabric.

I crept back and inhaled on Tor's joint before telling him what I had seen. He giggled and, after another pull, I joined him. The setting sun illuminated the smooth trunk and sparked from the offerings hanging above the honeyed surface of the waters. We laughingly discussed what the hell went on there. Birdsong crystallised in the far hedgerows and the only movement was from insects flitting through the shards of remaining light.

We were sharing another spliff when we noticed a rising mist and stars speckling the deepening sky. Bat calls strummed the field and the creatures flurried and swooped above us.

We licked a little more acid then prepared to settle down again. That's when the voices came. There were three, all talking at once. Two of them were clearly women, but the other was gruff and slurred its words.

We watched from behind a tree as two dishevelled women appeared by the water. They wore weathered military surplus gear and their long, dreaded hair was tied back. Both walked with a limp and one heaved at a large item. The growling thing was not visible. I tried not to giggle again as I imagined it a talking dog. The two knelt before the water. I parted the leaves for a better view. They reached into the pool and scooped out several items. They stood and then, talking softly, hung more ribbons from the branches. Then they left. That unseen thing growled on incoherently, sometimes breaking into groans of pain or delight.

Tor and I waited, listening, before I crept forward. I saw a brazier and a long, wooden box beside the water. The growling was coming from within that box.

As soon as I realised this, the thing fell silent, and I sensed unseen eyes upon me. There was a strange, pungent smell. Tor, wide-eyed, appeared beside me. I leaned over the box. It was made from old wood and had huge iron handles on its sides. I heard something breathing within it. I whispered, "Hello?" The breathing grew louder, and I could feel eyes boring through the wood and into me. I tested the lid, which pushed up easily. A horrible smell leaked out as I slowly opened it. Something snapped at my fingers, then the lid slammed shut and I fell into the marshy grass. The skin across my fingertips was torn. As blood welled from the cut, I was left thinking that a tiny person crammed into that box had bitten off the tips of my fingers.

I regained my footing and the voice rose again. This time, I could make out the words. "... your bones shall shine in his desert..."

As if in response, light fluttered through the treetops. I could hear the women's voices approaching again until the thing in the box began to shriek and howl. Tor had his head in his hands. By the time I got him to look up, the two women had their torches trained on us. The voice howled and groaned and the younger of the two kicked the box until it fell silent.

I explained that we had arrived by accident as the older woman drew closer and scanned us with her light.

"It's May full moon," she said. "You were meant to be here." Her words were slurred. When she beckoned us closer, I noticed that one of her hands was missing and that she had only three fingers on the other. "You won't be harmed; you were meant to see this." She had the gleam of the hallucinogenic mystic in her eyes.

The younger woman said, "Are these the ones Ma?" She resembled the older woman, and although she was also missing fingers, she was in possession of both hands.

"They might be, Arna." Ma studied Tor and me. "You like to get high? Yes? Want to see something that will really blow your mind? Want to feel something that will smash you into the stars?"

Tor, a glazed smile on his face, nodded. I offered them my LSD, but both refused. The younger woman, Arna, started a fire in the brazier, ignited a couple of burning brands, and then thrust them into the ground like medieval torches.

Ma pointed at the box, from which the murmuring had resumed. "She said you'd come with the May moon, old Nana in there, bless her. She was taught by her Nana and hers before her, that this pool of water on this little scrap of land of ours contains something special, something sacred.

"This patch of woods and marsh has been in the family for generations. It's no use for farming or building, but it suits us just fine." Ma levelled an unflinching gaze upon me before indicating the smooth trunk. "That is the remnant of a god who fell from the heavens and landed here."

"That's a dead tree," I said.

"No. It looks like a great, bare trunk, but its true nature is hidden. It is the vestige of a god who broke into time and space from the realm of timeless spirit, a god who reached out to us." She paused, staring intently, as if I should experience a sudden enlightenment. Tor nodded beside me; he must have licked more of the acid. The voice from the box chanted away.

Ma continued. "He took physical form and lived among us. He blew through the hollow bones of the dead, igniting his spark within them. He taught women how to bind bones so that they could host a trace of his presence. See? They hang around us like sparks cast from his blaze. Once his work was done, he cast aside his body. What you call a tree is a reminder of when he walked among us. We honour it and continue the rites that he taught, rites that have been passed down to us; along with the required sacrifices."

"So that is the corpse of a god?" I said.

Both women nodded and smiled. Arna took over. "The world out there will tell you that this is all there is," she gestured around, "or that the world of spirit is separate, but this dead trunk, this bone of a tree is a sign that he still reaches out to us. Bone is the dwelling of the eternal spirit: it outlives the flesh. When we reach out and leave one of our fragments with him, he reaches back. He enters into our souls. He summons us into eternity."

Ma revealed the stump of her missing arm. Under any other circumstances, it might be the start of a funny night with two women who clearly didn't need any more drugs. That's when Arna threw back the lid of the box and lifted out a stinking limbless person. She held the torso and head as if it were a baby then turned the thing so that it could see us. I could not tell if it was a man or woman that shrieked and chattered, its eyes rolling madly as it intoned to itself, "... beneath the water, within the slime, lie the bones... when life has withered, the bones last, desert-dry... the white heat of the god..."

Ma touched the woman's cheek. "My mother, our priestess, she is ready to begin her transition, her apotheosis. She predicted that tonight, when the May moon is in the sky, one would join us on the journey, one who would make a sacrifice."

The priestess yammered on. "The moon's piercing light opens our pathways to him..."

Ma drew a machete from her belt and held it in the firelight. "She will make her final sacrifice and pass into the eternity of his being."

Tor and I looked on in bewilderment whilst Arna laid the priestess down on the box so that her head extended over the water. Ma jabbed the blade toward me. "It is time for your journey to start."

I protested, but Arna reached out and grabbed me, then drew me toward the priestess, who called for the sacrifice to proceed.

Ma placed the blade in my hand. I didn't want to, I really didn't, but I was held fast and there was such a noise directed at me. I slashed down the blade. It thumped into the neck and released a spray of blood. The priestess screamed to her god for deliverance.

"We all have it in us," said Ma. "We have to reach down to it and let it out."

I swung again and hacked into a shoulder blade. The machete was stuck.

Arna steadied the torso with her foot, placed her hand over mine, and then levered the blade free. With a force I didn't think possible, she drove the blade down through the neck, silencing the creature and releasing a torrent of blood. She kicked off the head and held it aloft, thin strips dripping and dangling from it, before she tossed it – a muddied, deflated ball – into the water.

Ma reached skyward. "Lord dwelling beyond the world, draw near, reach through and inhabit this offering. Transform our inner selves into a desert through which your presence can burn. Arm us in the steel of your being!"

The head floated like a shrivelled apple and when it sank, it was down toward a soft glow patterning the bed of the pool. I felt that I was in the water, descending until I could see fragments of bone burning so vividly that they could have been constellations hanging in a void. I became aware too that the myriad of bones dangling from the trees cast an eerie luminescence among the foliage.

The two women, their faces misted in blood, stared down and chanted in hushed reverence. I could not hear their words. However, the atmosphere intensified and the still air stretched. The shards of bone burnt with greater intensity until the woods and the water around us fell away. The sky faded into blankness and only the trunk in the pond remained. It emitted a stark, clear light. Brighter and brighter still that light burnt until a great glare absorbed all in its immensity. I felt myself unravel.

When the light began to contract into shining orbs, something sparked and coiled within me. As they emerged into definition, the trees, the water, and even the faces of the women and Tor appeared to shine with droplets of light.

My body's aches returned and the cold air pinched at my skin. The light faded from the dead tree and broke into the reflection of firelight over the waves. I understood what the women had been talking about. I had been in the presence of such beauty that everything halted and all distinctions and barriers were burnt away. There could be no wealth or poverty, no belonging or vanishing, no life or death before such a being.

"She has gone from us now," said Ma. "She has returned to her true home."

Arna added, "The pact has been sealed; he has accepted you." She raised the blade.

"My time is drawing on apace," said Ma. "Moon by moon, I shall be initiated into his mysteries."

"I want..." I started.

"What? To be embraced in the fire of his being?" Ma held out her handless arm and looked into the pool. "Let me show you how. Arna."

Arna drew back the blade, then drove it down into Ma's elbow. Skin burst and bone shattered, throwing the older woman to the ground. Arna pressed the metal stump which had replaced her foot down on Ma's face, then swung twice more, hacking into the elbow.

Ma screamed. Her blood spattered the bone fragments hanging from the trees.

Arna twisted the forearm free, then applied fire to the wound. After a dedication, she offered the severed piece to the waters. The fire within me reignited and kept at bay the horror that should have seized me. I watched joyously as Ma, free of all pain, smiled.

When Arna cast another of her own fingers into the water, I felt the flame within me expand. In this strange state, I found myself nodding. Tor nodded too, a look of delirious wonder on his face.

Ma rose to her feet, then advanced with Arna. Tenderly, they took my hand and smoothed it out before extending my arm. I did not flinch as the blade plucked the smallest finger. My blood burned, but then that fragment seething within my core exulted and shedding its fleshy seal, rushed beyond the boundaries of the world.

When I arose, giggling and detached, I saw Tor offering his left hand.

"Let me," he whispered, "let me..."

The two smiled and Ma beckoned me with her remaining hand.

"Take the whole thing," said Tor. "I want to give it to him."

The blade was heavy, yet it spliced the air eagerly. Its joy filled me as I hefted it skyward and drove it down, hacking into Tor's wrist. He screamed and crumpled. Blood leaked from shattered bone as his hand was cast into the hungering water. Arna clamped his mutilated arm in hers and applied flame to the wound as he writhed and kicked in the grass.

The offerings traced their light over the branches above us and the bottom of the pool glowed once more. Each dangling bone exuded that radiance and my entire frame tingled. A sense of weightlessness came upon me and the exhilarating awareness that extinguished the distinction between my self and everything else took hold.

Tor's voice floated through my mind at some point. He had crawled to the edge of the pond and pointed into the water. "I see him."

The moon reflected smoothly across the surface until Tor dropped in headfirst and shattered that light. He splashed before plunging into the centre, where his silhouette was visible against the glare from below.

The world had broken into shining droplets gleaming against the night when Tor surfaced. He gasped and spat water before raising a sword. "He gave me this. His time has come."

He stood up in the water and stared at the blade whose gentle glow illuminated a certainty and determination that I had never seen in his face.

"Lori," he said, "the underside of that tree is rotted away and covered in weeds, but it looks like a face, a man's face. It spoke to me when I was in the water. It told me that it was not dead and that it needed our help to bring it back into this world. It offered me this sword that was tangled amongst the weeds. I didn't think anything could ever feel like this or be like this. The world has been smashed apart by something..."

"Something magical? Something fantastic?" I felt myself propelled toward the sword. The fire within me knew what had to be done.

"He needs more."

We killed the bouncers first. They were all gathered at the front gate where they snorted coke and looked at porn on their phones. I approached with a scalpel up my sleeve and acted like I was really out of it. Three of them laughed, but one was enraged for some reason. He opened the gates then stormed out as I backtracked. He managed to lay a hand on me before I slashed, opening the veins in his wrist. He went down on one knee and clutched the wound as a sheet of blood draped across him. He looked up. I jabbed the blade into an eye, then dug deep into the socket. My partners ambushed the remaining three. Ma, wielding a scythe in her remaining hand, slashed at the shins of two. Tor's sword felled the third before Arna set about all three with an axe. Their brief screams were drowned out by the shrieking laughter and music thumping from the party.

Mobile phone signals fell in and out around here, but Arna and Ma assured us that our devotions would be so quick that it would not matter if someone did manage to make a call before they felt the inner light. We skirted the shadows and identified where the guests were spread across the patio and pool area. The entry of the house was deserted, so Arna backed up a guest's Hummer until it blocked the front door. The pool area was surrounded by a high wall with one opening into it. Ma's scythe blocked this, thus trapping the teens inside whilst the three of us, intent on herding the guests into the house, circled the lawn.

When we heard the first of the screams from the pool and the guests' heads jolted around in disbelief, we knew it was time to act. None of the adults would ever know that Ma's scythe had plucked open a couple of teen abdomens, nor that the sight of bulging innards and pissing blood was enough to get the rest of the youngsters screaming and cowering in the corner of the pool whilst she stood on the terrace and swung the blade toward their faces.

Before any adults could investigate, Tor was among those on the lawn, his one-handed swordplay shredding the scattering guests. Arna and I hung back and made sure that any who fled the house lost at least their mobility. I had just noticed that the eyes of some our victims flared as if glimpsing the light that awaited them when the old man appeared from the kitchen with his gun...

Once all were dead, we hacked, prised, and peeled the flesh from their bones, reducing the lawn to a slick of punctured flesh and burst membrane. Although we slipped in the blood that the earth could not swallow and we tangled in uncoiled meat, it felt like every high I had ever taken had rushed back and sprung me out of my body. Neither horror nor regret touched me: our work was driven by a joyous abandonment of everything but that moment.

I was watching a fox snout-deep in a ribcage on the periphery of the massacre when Ma placed the torso of the priestess in the centre of the lawn. The hollow call of an owl suggested more night predators were arriving to feast.

As soon as Ma began to evoke the god, the priestess's ribs shuddered and flapped like wings. One by one, exposed bones around us popped and slipped free from their flesh to gleam in the moonlight. We all felt the luxurious, inward fire rekindle and I was dimly aware that his vast presence came amongst us. It moved across the remains like the wind over the sea. Its vastness set the earth shuddering. The world we had inhabited was an illusion before this being that burnt through ground and sky. As the lawn collapsed inward, dragging the broken bodies, the patio, and even the pool down into its depths, the point of fierce inner stillness, as bright as moonlight, swelled beyond the restraints of my body back toward its destiny. I felt myself elevated on warm wings, only dimly aware that the house shuddered and, in a flurry of splintering grass and snapping timbers, collapsed into a newly formed chasm to meet the onrushing sea. Nor was I alone; the white heat of others clustered exultantly around me, and entwined together we burnt free from what we had been.

And I felt Tor's presence. "Where you go," he said, "I will follow."

Beyond life's boundaries, we circled like suns in the piercing lightness of his being and the world we had known, the exclusion and the exploitation and the repression, was rendered a desert of shadow and bone.

M.S. Swift *writes horror and dark fantasy inspired by the ancient landscapes of the U.K. His contemporary horror tales have been published by Ghostwoods Books, the First United Church of Cthulhu,* Schlock! Webzine *and* Schlock! Bi-monthly. *He is currently working on a dark fantasy series inspired by the late medieval witch hunts, the first story of which has been published through Horrified Press. His long-term goal is to write a series of weird tales inspired by the early work of Wordsworth and Coleridge. He is paying off the accumulation of negative karma by working in the English education system.*

Quand les queues s'allongèrent

Antonella Coriander

When we heard the screams coming from Harriet's tent, we feared the worst. She was several months pregnant, with a child conceived *before*, and we all knew the risks. Mabel, beside me in the sleeping bag, dozed on, as if nothing was happening; for once I was envious of her poor hearing. I shook her awake before leaving our tent. There was no time for me to dress properly, but none of us slept in clothes that couldn't be worn on the run. Our world was like that then.

Other women were crowding around Harriet's tent, so many that I couldn't see in. There were twenty of us in the camp, which might seem a lot, but those were the only nineteen women that I knew to be alive in the world. We hoped that others had survived, but there was no way of knowing. None of us had a radio, and while a few solar chargers kept our phones going, there were no phone networks to connect them to.

We were camping in a supermarket loading bay, whose high fences had so far protected us from what was out there. Who knew if that safety would last? Our forays into the supermarket itself for food and water were fraught with danger, mad rushes to load a cart while swinging and cutting with hacksaws and knives and hoping to get out again before the spurting blood made the floor too slippery for us to escape. We had lost two women that way, two good women, Sunita and Tessa, caught and crushed by mindless yet living flesh.

"Let me through," I said to the other women at the tent. "I have some medical experience." I had been on a first aid training course, because it's important for librarians to know about things like that. You have no idea how many unconscious men and women I had to rouse from the stacks back in the day. There were no doctors or nurses in our group of survivors, so my certificate would have to do.

They made some space for me, and I knelt inside Harriet's tent. She was in a very bad state. Sweat poured from her forehead, her face grimaced in pain, and she clenched her fists, drilling them into the floor of the tent.

"Harriet," I said, as gently as I could while still speaking loudly enough to be heard, "I need to check your tummy. Is that okay?"

"Don't hurt my baby," she begged.

"I couldn't even if I wanted to," I said. "Is it your baby that is hurting you? When is its due date?"

"No, she's not due yet." Her eyes, tightly-closed, wept with the effort of containing the agony. "Not for months. She's all right. I'm all right. Just leave us alone."

I rested my hand on her belly. There was definitely movement, and more of it than I would have expected. I hadn't had a child of my own yet, but I remembered putting my hand on my mother's belly when she was pregnant with my younger sister, and that had been nothing like this. That had been a kick here and there, at most an arm being swept across beneath the surface, but this was... I don't know... roiling was the only word for it.

"Are you sure it's a girl?" I tried to say it kindly,

though time was short, in my estimation. "Did you have a scan?"

She nodded. "Yes, it is a girl. There was nothing on the scan."

From the activity in her belly, I had my doubts. I left the tent, and Mabel took my place, holding Harriet's hand and wiping her brow with what I recognised as my gym towel. When it had all gone wrong, one Thursday evening in July, I had been on my way back from the gym. If it hadn't have been for my Nike trainers, I'd have been dead, like all the other women who died that night, but I ran, ran as fast as I could, and found other women who were running, and we made it here. That had been five weeks ago, and we were starting to think about what would happen when the weather got worse in autumn. We had survived a few summer showers, but we were not equipped for the cold of an October, much less a December.

The rest of the group gathered around me.

"It's bad," I told them. "And I don't know what we can do."

"Could the baby be delivered?" asked Maggie, who had been a manager at this supermarket. Her knowledge of its layout had been invaluable during our attempts to acquire food and camping gear – the latter a special promotion right by the front doors. An end-stack had saved our lives.

I shook my head. "It's far too early for that. And it's a boy, I'm sure of it. I can feel what's happening through the skin of her belly. She's trying to tough it out, but we all know what's coming."

"She's going to die," said Maggie. "Unless we get it out of her."

"No!" Harriet was standing outside her tent, both hands clutching her swollen belly. "You won't take my baby! You won't!"

It must have been the pain driving her mad. She

knew as well as we did what was happening. To her, to the baby. She tried to run, but where could she have run to? Beyond the gates the way was blocked, like everything was blocked, and high walls blocked everywhere else, to keep out thieves in the old days, to keep out danger now. And she was in no state to run anyway.

She took a few staggering steps towards the gate, and that was as far as she ever got. She fell to the ground, screaming in agony, clutching her belly, ripping at her T-shirt as if that would help. We knew it wouldn't.

"Get your weapons," I said quietly to the women closest to me. They passed the message on to others, and we did our best to ignore the wails of anguish as we gathered up what we had in the way of fighting gear. It wasn't much. I had a large cooking knife and thought myself lucky. Others had small hacksaws, razors and corkscrews.

Harriet was no longer in control of her body. She was thrown about like a rag doll by the thing growing uncontrollably within her, twisted from side to side, her arms and legs powerless, useless appendages to her swelling, writhing, bubbling torso.

"Please, kill me now," she whimpered. "I can't stand it any more."

She didn't have to. At that moment her belly broke open and out boiled an ever-lengthening, endlessly unspooling baby penis, the force of its emergence ripping Harriet to bits, showering us with her blood, and bringing her suffering to a merciless end.

The disaster was not over. It was happening now to the next generation. We still don't know what triggered it. Evolution? Mutation? Radiation? No rescue helicopters ever came, so we assumed it had affected the entire world. It had almost seemed funny when it first happened.

That's what I thought about as I chopped away at the stretching stem, before it could do to us what it had done to Harriet.

On that Thursday evening in July, the men's pants had started to bulge, just a little at first, which was gross but slightly amusing, and then they had all fallen to the ground as the growth became uncontrollable, the weight unbearable, and their penises had burst from their trousers.

That's why I felt no joy in slashing and cutting at the thin thing that now threatened us. I knew it wasn't malicious in itself; it was barely even aware of us. It just had to grow, it was following an unconscious biological imperative, but unless we fought back it wouldn't leave any space for us to live.

As quickly as we hacked and sawed and cut away at it, leaving chunks of tiny penis scattered over the ground like little pink slugs, it grew back, longer and longer, unstoppable in its quest to take up every possible space it could find. I couldn't bring myself to attack the tiny baby itself, the little creature silently screaming at the root of the monstrous growth, buried in its mother's guts, but if I didn't do something we would all be dead in minutes.

I ran to Harriet's remains, ducking beneath the briar tangle of baby flesh, and cut at the stem as close to the boy as I could. I picked him up, gave him a kiss for luck, then tossed him over the wall that protected us from all the other raging penises. His was already growing back before he was out of my arms, and through the grille of the yard gate I saw it lower him gently to the ground. He'd be all right. It was the least I could do for Harriet, and I knew it wasn't enough.

Once the men were in this state they didn't seem to need food. We had seen the way their bodies settled into the ground, relaxing ever more while their penises waved in the air like tall thin triffids. In later years we even noticed the colour of the members changing, acquiring a greenish tint. Chlorophyll, we thought. Maybe photosynthesis was how they stayed alive.

The men were no longer conscious, at least not in the way we understood it. On the rare occasions that we were able to see their faces, buried as they were beneath their own knotted willies, they looked happy but stupid, lost in the pleasant reverie that came from giving in to the desire to be nothing but unthinking, unrestrained cocks.

Although we survived the incident with Harriet and her baby, we couldn't stay there in the supermarket. Looking back, I'm glad it got us moving. Most of us made it here, though I still miss Maggie. Onto the canals and into barges, at first, then down near the coast and onto this island. There weren't many men here when it happened, and we cleared away those that were, sheltering in the barges at night, moving on to the land once it was safe.

Now we're self-sufficient. We grow our own vegetables, and have fresh water to drink. Meat, of course, is plentiful. We even began to have babies again, and that's where you came along. We milk the – well, we think of them as baby-plants now, more than men. And while there's still the risk that our children will be boys, we can test for that early and perform an emergency caesarean before they really start to grow. It's still dangerous, but we think it's worth the risk. The boys are taken off the island, and the girls grow up here.

If we want anything else from the mainland, we still have to fight our way through the forest of cocks, through the crowds of unfettered, conscienceless manhood. But isn't that exactly what we had already been doing for thousands of years? And we will keep fucking doing it forever till women can live in peace.

Antonella Coriander *has previously contributed eight episodes of her Oulippean serial, Les aventures fantastiques de Beatrice et Veronique, to this magazine. The French title of her story in this volume translates to "when the queues got longer" (as in a supermarket, where the action takes place). But in French "queues" is also a word for willies.*

The Fisherman's Ring

Drew Tapley

The procession circled the Vatican wall, with hundreds of dignitaries heading the line. If you stood outside St Peter's Basilica when the parade approached, it was at least an hour before you caught sight of the cardinals.

Nine days of official mourning followed the death of Pope Johan Innocent VII. When the College of Cardinals was called to elect a new Pope, the entire world engaged in debate over who would succeed him.

Cardinal Edvard Steinhoffman of Austria was the favoured successor, but really, it was anyone's guess. Only the Holy See knew the exact system of selection. It had been this way in the Roman Catholic Church since the fourteenth century: an election process steeped in secrecy and myth.

The Parade of the Cardinals was a recent addition to boost the Church's social media presence, and had garnered much global attention.

After the one hundred and twenty cardinals entered the papal conclave, they would remain locked inside for days of discussion over who should become the next successor of St Peter.

As the parade turned into the Vatican grounds, the cardinals' vestments formed a block of scarlet approaching the Sistine Chapel. Huge golden doors were pulled apart for them to enter, and were closed with a hefty bolt. The world prepared to wait. For the next three days, no one would enter or leave those doors.

An anchorwoman standing outside the entrance adjusted her position to keep the afternoon sun, reflecting off the doors, from hitting the camera lens.

"The emergence of black smoke from this chimney over here means that voting is still in session," she said. "However, when a new Pope has been elected by a two-thirds majority, white smoke will appear, the bells of St Peter's Basilica will ring, and all eyes will be on the central balcony to receive the new Holy Father."

The Catholic Church and all its supporters stood on ceremony. The meter was running.

Inside the Sistine Chapel, Cardinal Alfonso scowled, and the cigarette between his lips spat ash each time he jerked his head. Cardinal Almeida's face, on the other hand, strained under extreme effort and dripped with sweat. His mitre sat on the back of his head, and his chest was as red as his vestment robes that lay on the floor between him and Alfonso. This was the most intense titty twister Cardinal Alfonso had dished out to a fellow senior cleric.

Chief adjudicator Cardinal Vascos held his thumb over a stopwatch and scrutinized both men. With a mighty grunt, Cardinal Almeida slapped his hand repeatedly on the table to tap out for a time of four minutes and twelve seconds. Thirty seconds above Cardinal Marcus. That put Cardinal Almeida in second place overall.

"Well done," said Cardinal Vascos. "Now switch over."

While Cardinal Alfonso disrobed and Cardinal Almeida applied cream to his nipples, Cardinal Vascos ambled over to a large whiteboard and entered the recorded time on a chart with over a hundred names and dozens of activities. He walked past a line-up of cardinals standing before an adjudicator, who was kneeling in front of them with a tape measure. Cardinal Carmen unbuttoned his robe from hip to knee as the adjudicator leaned in with the tape measure.

"Three point two inches," he said to an assistant with a clipboard.

"Are you sure?" said Cardinal Carmen. "Do it again. One more time."

The adjudicator rolled his eyes and measured again. "Three point *one* inch. My mistake. Next."

Cardinal Carmen schlepped away as the next in line moved forward. The adjudicator leant in then immediately sat back on his haunches. The tape measure snaked back to base with a loud click. With venom in his eyes, he stared up at the competitor. "I said SOFT!"

The slurping and cheering nearby were enough to distract the other cardinals from their events. Everyone thought Cardinal Aurelius would excel at competitive eating, but when they laid the seventh plate of chicken wings under his nose, the sixth was already on its way back up. Aurelius had gone too hard too fast with no thought for strategy. Cardinal Philippe of Chile cleaned off his seventh plate and tossed the bone ceremoniously over his shoulder. It was a classic tale of the hare and the tortoise.

The large room divided into cubicles of activity, all tallied on the central whiteboard. Finding the most capable Bishop of Rome required testing all manner of physical and mental endurance.

Candidates made their way from event to event during day one, which included scheduled meal breaks and an evening off to watch Juventus against Real Madrid.

Crowds gathered around the chimney at five o'clock to see what colour the smoke would be.

Cardinal Vascos carefully rounded the scores and

entered them in the grand total column. He used a calculator with keys so large he had to press two fingers onto each one. His eyes were definitely not what they were when he was only eighty-two.

Once the scores were published, the cardinals assembled to determine if there was a clear winner. Cardinal Alfonso led at the close of the first day, but it was not enough to secure him as the Holy Father.

The world waited, all eyes on the roof of the Sistine Chapel. Inside, dozens of full ashtrays were dumped into a roaring fireplace. A plume of black smoke rose up the stack and funnelled out the chimney. Day one concluded with no Pope. And the world went to bed.

On the morning of day two, eager participants inundated the burp-the-alphabet event. So it was that after a full day of events, and an early night following a 2–1 win to Juventus, the cardinals were eager to prove their skill with the controlled exhalation of trapped air. Vascos certainly didn't anticipate the turnout, and had to order another crate of beer. He checked his watch. A load of dirty diapers would be coming in about now.

This was the least popular event, and most cardinals skipped it. Not all events were mandatory, and some, like this one, came with double points for those lagging behind.

Cardinal O'Reilly, for instance, scored poorly on the press-ups and the wrestling, and thought he should have done better at lighting his farts after lunch yesterday. However, he did just manage to amplify his score on burp-the-alphabet, and felt encouraged to double up. He strapped on the gas mask while Vascos emptied several garbage bags of soiled diapers into an industrial drum, then sealed the lid with duct tape. One end of a rubber venting tube bore into the lid, and the other attached to the snout of O'Reilly's gas mask.

No one had managed more than a minute, and Cardinal O'Reilly should have put more consideration into the order of his day. After a hearty breakfast and litres of fizzy beer, he barely cleared ten seconds before barfing into the mask. Despite Vascos's poor eyesight and escalating years, he was surprisingly quick on his feet. He ripped off the mask as barf began to fill the eyeholes.

After that, and in view of the fight at the poker table the previous day, Vascos decided to add a few more rules to the tournament.

As always, the egg and spoon race was a riot. Somehow, Cardinal Martinez had sneaked in a larger spoon and was arguing with Vascos over his disqualification. They had to call over the adjudicator with the tape measure to settle the debate, and discovered that the spoon was twice the regulation size. After his intolerable language during charades, Martinez was officially declared persona non grata and asked to leave the conclave via a back door.

When this second day of events came to a close, no clear winner emerged. The world was informed.

Everyone got into the swing of it for day three. The energy was up and candidates were eager to demonstrate their aptitude.

After some flagrant cheating at arm wrestling, another cardinal was shown the back door. Vascos needed eyes in the back of his head to add to the failing ones in the front. Over the last fifty years, the Holy Father was always declared on the third day, and it seemed that the enthusiasm for outright cheating was redoubled in view of this fact. Vascos was being summoned from one event to another when adjudicators could no longer contain a fight, or the size of someone's mother had been introduced into an argument.

Thank God for the body waxing event to calm everyone down. Having hair ripped from flesh takes the wind out of anyone's sails... even high-ranking, world-renowned theologians.

Candidates lay on a massage table while fellow candidates applied, then tore off wax strips. A highly sensitive microphone logged even the slightest squeak, so the trick was to seal your mouth and breathe through your nose. It also helped to grip the chrome handles.

Cardinal Marcus had done well on his chest and legs, but started screaming before the strips could be applied between his inner thighs. It was considered to be in his best interest not to proceed, as it was for Cardinal Dimitri, who had more hair that a Himalayan yak.

The candidates took an afternoon break to focus on the closing event of day three: the chilli pepper contest. Of the one hundred and twenty candidates who walked through those golden doors three days ago, six had been disqualified, two were in solitary confinement (mostly for their own protection), one had abdicated, and another was taken to the local hospital. This left one hundred and ten in the running.

Trestle tables were set into classroom rows, with buckets of ice-cold water and milk placed along each one. This was the oldest and most esteemed event in the history of the College of Cardinals. It was so old, in fact, that legend spoke of a Cardinal Antonio who, in 1683, imbibed thirty-eight Thai dragon peppers. It was also widely documented that Cardinal Antonio could speak to animals and had two hearts, so that story was under historical investigation with Church administrators.

Vascos carried the Naga King Chilli in a jar, and placed it on a separate table at the front of the room. Cultivated by the Naga people of Northeast India, it is often ranked as the world's hottest chilli pepper. Folklore has it that the Naga people once used it to boil the skin off human skulls from rival tribes.

The cardinals took their seats and prayed. Vascos looked at the leaderboard. There were two frontrunners: Cardinal Leopoldo Ramirez of Colombia, and Cardinal Edvard Steinhoffman of Austria. It could go either way, and both men knew their performance in this event would be the deciding vote. They glanced across the room and found each other's eyes.

Outside St Peter's Basilica, crowds packed in. Day three expectations soared.

Adjudicators walked down the rows and used tongs to drop chillies into bowls. They would continue doing so until there were either no candidates or no chillies remaining. That was at least what the rules stated. Those who could no longer continue excused themselves and waited on beanbags at the rear of the room while clutching chalices of ice water or milk. Others had to be forcefully removed when they either stopped breathing or turned the same colour as the pepper they were attempting to swallow.

Milk and chilli seeds covered the floor. Those who skipped drinking with hopes of saving precious seconds were the first ones out.

There was a clear strategy to this. Chew. Breathe. Drink. Swallow. Repeat. Only thirty-one made it to the end, and the Vatican physician had to intervene twice. Everyone now looked to the leaderboard as Vascos made the scores official.

At the end of day three, Steinhoffman and Ramirez were deadlocked as majority leaders. You couldn't slide

a postage stamp between their scores; and they
accepted the inevitable.

Outside St Peter's, not a single car engine
challenged the silence. Millions around the world
awaited the smoke.

Vascos brought the jar to the table where both
cardinals sat opposite each other. He clamped the
tongs around the monster chilli pod that resembled an
aging rock star with sunken jowls, sagging skin, and
hollow eyes. Ramirez reared like a horse. Steinhoffman
turned away. The room waited. The world waited.

Ramirez used the tongs to lift the chilli, and
inspected its gnawed recesses. He knew that the
longer he waited, the worse it would be, so he bit off a
small piece at the pointed end. A chorus of revulsion
echoed around the room.

All the moisture disappeared from Ramirez's mouth
in an instant. Because the rules of this round barred
drinking any fluids, he flipped his head to toss the
infernal piece to the back of his throat. It scratched
and clawed its way down to his gullet, and those close
by could hear his stomach acid screaming. But it was
down. Ramirez dropped the remaining chilli pod in a
gold bowl, laid the tongs across it, and slid it to his
opponent.

Steinhoffman beat a fist against his breastplate three
times. He lifted the chilli with the tongs, and a few
loose seeds hung down like poisoned testicles. He
closed his eyes and bit into the open base, then tore
away a tiny piece.

Holding it centrally in his mouth, he summoned
saliva from every crook. It burned into his tongue, so
he transferred it to the roof of his mouth but instantly
tried to scrape it off with the tip of his numb tongue.
Seconds ticked by. He had to get it down his throat
quickly, or else out of his mouth. Seeds were coming
loose and fusing to his cheeks. He started to convulse,

and reached one hand for water, but then pulled it back with his other hand. It was too much for some cardinals, who left the room. Others whispered to each other, but most were pinned to the scene.

The Austrian cardinal placed his head on the table for a whole minute. When he lifted it, he looked like the devil himself with piercing red eyes and blue veins engorged on his forehead and neck. Vascos used a chalice to scoop up some milk, which he forced down Steinhoffman's throat. Two more cardinals came in and held him steady while the physician took his pulse. It was over. Everyone knew it, especially Ramirez, who held his hands aloft like a prize fighter and screamed in triumph. He slapped Steinhoffman hard on the back, which dislodged the pepper fragment from the roof of his mouth and into a puddle of milk.

In the communal showers, a fresh cork popped every few minutes. You couldn't tell the difference between champagne and shampoo, and the cardinals amused themselves by chanting and slapping each other on the ass. Ramirez, periodically hoisted up like a trophy, was right in the middle of it.

Vascos fired up the barbeque by the fireplace, and lined the grill with prime steaks. White smoke filled the chimney stack and rose high into the evening sky. The world reacted.

The men were still singing and popping corks well beyond the first jubilant hour. Vascos had to turn off the water at source to get them out. His Holy Father was towel-dried, dressed, and presented with the Pope's signet ring: The Ring of St Peter the Fisherman.

As Deacon of the College of Cardinals, Cardinal Vascos stepped onto the Vatican balcony before billions of people awaiting the official announcement. From a respectful distance, you could barely see the bags under his eyes caused by three days of continuous stress. He composed himself, summoned what little strength he had, and smiled.

"Habemus Papam!" he said in Italian, and then again in English. "We have a Pope!"

The gathered crowds roared as the newly-appointed Supreme Pontiff appeared on the balcony next to Vascos to deliver his apostolic homily to the waiting world.

He opened his arms wide and spoke in accented Italian. A large digital board underneath him transcribed his words into English.

"My brothers and sisters, I stand before you in honour and privilege as the new Holy Father of the largest church in Christianity. These past few days have provided an invaluable perspective into the deep psychological and physical trials one must expect of this role.

"After almost sixty years of theological and spiritual training, the last few days of intense self-reflection have provided the strongest fortification of my enduring faith, and have prepared my vision to lead this Church.

"Let us now unite in love, in purpose, and in prayer to serve His word, support the sick, poor, and afflicted, and continue the strong foundation of interfaith dialogues to spread His mercy and acceptance throughout the world."

As the sun went down over the Vatican that evening, the hopes and dreams of the Church rose high. The gathered crowds looked up at the Vatican balcony, and followed their new Pope in prayer.

Drew Tapley is a copywriter and journalist, and has been publishing in Canada, Australia, and his native England for the last decade, both in print magazines and journals, as well as online. He is now based in

Toronto, and has been making short films for the last five years. Some of his films have screened at film festivals throughout the world. He was recently published in the UK's Popshot Magazine, *and has two published books: one fiction, and one nonfiction.*

The Armageddon Coat

Howard Watts

---

1. Jacket

His breathing was rapid now, his heart pounding. He could have committed so many more acts, but that all got fucked up by his capture and conviction.

"It's all going to shit anyways," he shouted, "and you knows it, yo'all can read, right? You know all this manufactured crap you call reality is just one great fucking lie. That's why they're all making and taking as much as they can, pushing down the little guy, climbing up over everybody, exploiting them. They're livin' behind their high walls, their gated homes while outside the world turns to shit, all because of them."

They watched from behind the glass. Morbid, fascinated, aroused. Transfixed? Some. Unable to look away, waiting for it.

He smelled the disinfectant now, then crapped himself. There was the muttered order, then the sharp click as the drug was released. The liquid coursed through the plastic tube, toward where it had been spliced into his vein. Moments now. Behind the glass, they shuffled in anticipation, some leaning forward, squinting. He began to scream for mercy and that's what they wanted to hear, wanted to ignore. They wanted him to see this, and he did, smiling back at them in finality. Every person in the room believed he'd won.

Jeff tore off the dirty jacket, then threw it into the dark and dusty corner of the basement room. He scrambled away from the experience. "Holy fuck, that was intense! That was great – best yet!" Shaking, he wiped the sweat from his eyes, then ran his hands over his shaved head. He pointed at the jacket. "You gotta try that. It's so fucking cool!"

Glynis, arms folded, stood in the doorway. "I keep telling you, don't cuss!" She took a few steps forward. "You said it was my turn first. Liar!"

"I found the place," Jeff thumbed his chest, "so it's *my* call." He snatched up the jacket, then threw it at her. "Go on then. Your turn, Glyn. Try it. It's better than that bus driver's cap you found last week, even though the crash was kinda cool."

She smelled the death woven into its thick cotton threads, the musty odour of dust and remnants of stale days long past. "Bet it's not as good as that whore's shawl I found you. You really got off on that." She folded the jacket.

Jeff, passing the disjointed pile of bones that was once the jacket's owner, marched over to her. "That was your fault. You should know by now – no sharing clothes. Never together!"

She ignored his anger and spoke matter of fact. "You enjoyed it, admit it."

He took the jacket, dropped it on the floor, and then, with hands by his sides, kissed her quickly on the cheek. She looked him in the eyes for a moment, then kissed him back. They both tasted dust... the death of billions, breaking down into trillions upon trillions of organic remains hanging in the heavy atmosphere.

The few remaining scientists posited that the bombs had been placed by aliens long ago. These beings could no longer experience emotions and so they watched us and, when our behaviour became so deplorable, they detonated the bombs that somehow embedded memories, experiences, and emotions into non-organic materials from which the aliens could experience everything humanity left behind.

Many wanted to believe this explanation, but couldn't. Blame was instantly levelled across continents and oceans to foreign shores, and retaliation came swiftly by man's own hand. Those who had survived the aliens' first strike cast decimation upon the Earth. Now the few remaining trigger men presided over the dust, amid their kingdoms of catastrophe, governed from the safety of their subterranean castles as the survivors sought food, water, and answers. The triggermen have since seen the aliens... walking through the rubble, caressing the walls, and absorbing the memories fused there. But seeing was not believing for these men, for even now they are too stupid to admit their errors. Excuses came forth quicker than any apology or admission of guilt. "I did it to take them with us." "It was the correct decision." "If I had to make that choice again, it wouldn't change."

Jeff had found out by accident shortly after the bombs went off two years ago. Cold and alone, he fended off torrential rain in a ruined house on the outskirts of Boston. He shivered in a foetal ball on a stained bed that injected memories of a young woman's tragic life. It changed him, ruined his innocence with the memory of her reality, of an adult's life. He stood and the memories remained, but they had ceased entering him. He climbed back into the bed and they continued to flow into him; he understood. Then in the morning, Jeff, a child no more, had cut away a small stained part of the pillow. It was a map of part of her life that he sometimes held against his cheek during the night. His private comfort, his escape.

He had found Glynis crying, hungry, and alone in her house. He gave her a hit from the clothes, helped her through her first experience of another's life. She loved him for that, for taking her in and not taking from her what he wanted and then leaving her alone as others had. He made her feel the future was worthwhile, and showed her the present could be lived through with the memories of the past. They were inseparable.

---

2. Shoes

Jeff headed for the execution room exit. "So where to next?"

"DC. I wanna go to DC. Never been there – I was promised a few times by my dad." Glynis scooped up the jacket and chased after him. "But we never did. Always South Carolina. Mom always visiting her family. I hated that, hated her family. My cousin was a fat idiot, calling me stupid names and laughing at me because I didn't like going into the ocean."

Jeff stopped in the doorway and thought for a moment. "Okay, Washington it is."

The day was grey and blue, softened by silence, hardened by the landscape. Rubble crowded the edges of the road. They took to their bikes and rode, Jeff's pulling a squeaking cart containing the garments they had collected and neatly folded. He unfolded a map. "We'll take the George Washington Memorial Parkway once we reach Alexandria. Should take a couple a' days."

Silent streets. The outskirts of Alexandria were carefully measured subdivisions. Blocks of narrow, once colourful houses, chain-link fences rusting around them as if to cage the bones of the dead hidden behind the crumbling walls and broken windows. Telegraph poles wilting against the sky. Burnt out cars, two out of each ten a hearse.

"How come the others don't collect the clothes?" said Glynis as she pulled alongside Jeff.

He shrugged. "They're adults. They've had their lives, I guess."

"So you're saying they don't get the hit off them?"

"I don't think they can. If they did, they'd be collecting them too."

Glynis thought for a moment. "But then if these aliens are so, so old, how come *they* can get a hit off of what's left?"

"I dunno, Glyn," he said. "Maybe they're still young, like us. Maybe even though they've been here millions of years, maybe they're still kids too."

"Maybe they never grow up."

"Who'd fucking want to?"

The trees lining the street were full of leaves, and as the breeze brushed them together, Glynis was reminded of the sound of the tide against the South Carolina coast. She peddled faster to escape the sounds and the memory, but kept her eyes out for an overlooked bone pile by the side of the road. She wanted to find a pair of ballet shoes. She'd tie them tightly around her feet, then spread her toes. Her mother refused to pay for ballet lessons – too old-fashioned, too expensive – but for her it was a dream she could perhaps live through someone else's life. She stopped. "Can I look at the map a minute?"

Jeff handed it over. "What ya looking for?"

"A ballet school."

He smiled, sat back in the saddle, and folded his arms. "You wanna be a fucking ballet dancer eh? Jumping and spinning around the floor to some boring old muzak?"

She looked up to him without lifting her head. "It's called a ballerina, jerkoff – and stop cussing! So what if I am?" She placed her hands on her hips and steadied the bike on tiptoes. "And what about you, what are you after in Washington? You never let me choose where we go. You're always saying because you're a year older, you know best. You sound like my mom used to sometimes."

"I'll be a teenager my next birthday, so that'll make me more in charge. I know what's best for us."

"You didn't answer me." She handed back the map. "What are you after?"

He folded it and placed it under his T-shirt. "I wanna find a spacesuit in a museum, a real used spacesuit."

She raised her eyebrows and shook her head before peddling off. "You don't even know when your birthday is!"

The Centre de Danse on Prospect Street was a small building next to an antique shop. From the outside, the terracotta walls with grey shuttered windows looked nothing like any ballet school that Glynis had ever imagined. There should have been a large bay window with mannequins wearing leotards and pointe shoes, white silk with cream ribbons, tutus of fine netting. The mannequins would be posing: one in an arabesque, another in a first position plié.

"This it?" Jeff sipped from his water bottle, then passed it to her.

"It's what your map says."

"Well come on then. Let's get inside, get a pair of shoes, and get out of here. We're low on tinned stuff." He looked to the sky. "It'll be dark and cold in less than half an hour."

Behind the inner black panelled door with its faded brass fittings, the reception desk was surprisingly tidy. Pens in a Centre de Danse mug, a diary left open, an empty bottle of sparkling water, a pile of elastic hair ties. Beyond, the small dance hall was bright. Framed pictures and certificates were carefully arranged upon the walls, but the large mirror above the two-tiered barre was cracked with ugly jagged lines, reminding Glynis of the summer lightning she'd seen off the coast of Charleston many years ago.

Jeff peered down the dark stairway set behind the wall holding the mirror. "Might be a locker room down there?" He activated a wind-up LED torch from his backpack to illuminate the stairs.

In the cramped basement, small pigeon holes with colourful name tags dominated the far wall. Glynis noticed some ballet shoes and walked over.

"Hurry up, Glyn. We don't have a lot of time."

She pulled a pair of shoes from a box. "It's safe here – we could stay the night and search for food in the morning? No one's gonna shack up in a ballet school. There's no food or stuff to take."

Jeff investigated the remaining walls. There were chairs with children's clothes draped over them, piles of bones, cell phones, soft toys, and a few small backpacks with cartoon characters emblazoned upon them. "Looks like they were getting ready when the bomb went off," he said as the torchlight explored the details. "I guess you're right. We'll stay the night. Hurry up and find the shoes you want. I'll start unloading the cart and bring the stuff and bikes in." He took another torch from his backpack. "Here. Take this. It'll be dark soon."

She nodded, replacing the shoes that were a couple of sizes too small for her, then wound the torch and listened to Jeff climb the stairs as she searched the other pigeon holes.

Night had fallen. Jeff, standing in the doorway, turned off the torch and scanned the streets for movement. The late summer breeze had moved on and everything was as still as a photograph. Satisfied, he hurried to the cart and picked up a pile of clothes.

In the basement Glynis found a brightly painted wooden door under the stairway, with a small toilet and wash basin beyond. The torchlight fell against the basin, where a bar of slimy white soap sat in a small pool of water next to the hot tap. The torchlight moved to the toilet. A thick clear liquid refracted the light. It clung to the porcelain in suspended waves and as she bent down to take a closer look, the smell of bleach greeted her. She stood, relieved by the sound of footsteps coming down the stairs above her head. "Think the toilet's still working, Jeff."

Jeff, still on the ground level, heard Glynis just as a figure jumped from the shadows of the dance hall and said, "Just where do you think you're going with that?"

Jeff dropped the clothes. The point of a long carving knife was at his throat.

Glynis felt the toilet door move behind her and touch her back. "Don't play tricks, Jeff." But the door slammed into Glynis and knocked her into the cramped toilet room where she fell against the rear wall with a painful thud. "What the hell are you doing?" She struggled to her feet.

A woman's voice came from the other side of the door. "Stay put, sweetheart." There was the sound of a chair being dragged across the floor, then wedged under the door handle. Glynis pushed and kicked at the door, but it wouldn't budge.

"I got her, Cliff!" shouted the woman. "Gonna get at least two months' supplies for this one. Pretty little thing."

Upstairs Jeff took a step back as his adversary moved the knife between his hands. The man was in his late forties Jeff estimated, and looked kempt considering the situation. "Relax, son. Don't do anything stupid and this will go nice and easy for us both. My name's Cliff."

"I got that already. What do you want, Cliff?"

"We want you to relax. Just lay on the floor with your hands behind your back and everything will be okay."

"You want supplies? We don't have any, just the clothes, a couple a' tins, and one bottle of water. That's all."

"Been collecting memories have you son?" Cliff grinned and glanced at the pile of rags between them. "Getting off on others' lives, huh?"

"It keeps us off the streets." Jeff continued circling to the left.

"Don't seem fair to me." Cliff maintained his position facing Jeff. "Nothing left for the adults, just the rubble and you freaky kids. You two will keep us fed for three months at least, once you're sold off to the needy."

"Now that's not nice, mister." Jeff raised his voice. "My sister's not of age yet – but if you let us go, we'll help you."

"Really? And how do you figure that?"

"We've got a lot of memories in those clothes, know where a few of the local government underground food stashes are. What's that worth to you?" Jeff held up his palms, fingers apart. "I'll show you." He bent slowly to the clothes. "Gotta great jacket here somewhere, found it in a government building about a mile away. Must've cost a fortune: tags are written in Italian, I think. Guy must've been some kinda important dude for sure."

"Slowly son." Cliff waved the knife. "I'm prepared to take a loss of payment if I have to slice your pretty face."

"No need, no need, Cliff. Just let me find the jacket." Jeff rummaged in the pile. "It's here somewhere. Maybe my sister left it outside on the cart. Then I can take you to the nearest stash – where we were gonna head to in the morning."

Cliff studied Jeff for a few seconds, then shouted, but kept his eyes on the boy. "You all right down there Ruth?"

"No problems," came the woman's voice. "What's the holdup?"

"Nothing to worry about, but the deal may have just got a whole lot sweeter. Bring the girl upstairs and give me a minute." Cliff sighed, thinking things through. "Okay son, let's move slowly outside and find that jacket."

"Whatever you say."

Downstairs Glynis heard movement behind the door. "I'm going to let you out now sweetheart. Behave yourself and you'll be fine."

"Forgot to mention." Jeff walked down the outside steps to the cart. "There's a shawl from a whore somewhere in that pile. Wore it myself. If you tie it around my sister for a night, she'll be worth more to you with those memories, perhaps double, perhaps enough to let *me* go, considering the experiences she'll have?"

"You're a real dealer son, aren't you?"

"If it's a case of me getting fucked over and over again or her, it's a no brainer. I'll take you to the first food stash, dig out the whore's shawl, and we can part ways. Deal?"

"Sounds fair."

Jeff rummaged around the pile of clothes as Glynis and Ruth appeared at the doorway.

Ruth said, "Is this going to take long?"

"Here it is." Jeff looked up to Glynis and nodded. Then he pulled on the jacket from the execution room. A murderous rage coursed through him. A memory voice screamed in his head. *"Slice me, sell me, fuck me, kill me? No chance buddy, you don't know what you got comin'."* He picked up a pile of clothes and threw them in Cliff's face, then kicked him between the legs. Cliff fell to his knees, but Jeff kept kicking, over and over again, as hard as he could until his foot hurt.

Glynis, stretching on tiptoes, thrust her bleach-soaked hands into Ruth's eyes, then pushed with her thumbs as hard as she could. The woman screamed and Glynis pushed against her chest, sending her stumbling back into the dance hall.

Jeff had the knife now, and with a swift movement sliced into the man's cheek. The blade cut deep and took off the tip of his nose. The bloody stump fell to the ground and Cliff didn't know whether to clutch his cheek or pick up the tip from the dust. That moment of indecision was all Jeff needed. He stabbed Cliff's left thigh. "Move back into the building, now!" *"Yo'all thinks you're gonna watch me die, huh? Gonna sees me go? No way you fuckers. I'm outta that chair, coming for ya, gonna punish ya'll."*

Cliff, scrambling backward up the steps as best he could, held his cheek and nose with one hand as they coursed with crimson. He screamed, "You little shit."

"Don't fuck with me!" Jeff sent spit into the air. *"Got ya now, asshole, your time's a coming, that's for sure, gonna make ya pay."* Jeff struggled to push back the memories from the execution room jacket and focus on the now. "Hurry up Cliff, you're leaving a mess on the steps. Get on with it." He picked up the tip of Cliff's nose and placed it in his trouser pocket.

Inside, Ruth was still screaming and clawing at her eyes as she lay on her back. Glynis, breathing hard, feeling guilty, stood over her and stared at her hands. She heard Jeff.

"Cliff, help her up and get downstairs. Carry her if you have to. Move!" Jeff brought up the knife again, but Cliff held up a trembling bloodied hand for mercy. He wiped away strands of clotted blood and snot dangling from his nose. "Okay, okay, give me a chance."

Within minutes, Ruth and Cliff were in the toilet under the stairway.

"I'll come for you, kid," said Cliff. "Trust me, you better be watching because when I get hold of you and her I'm gonna make sure you both live just long enough to understand what real pain's all about."

"*Gotta cut him deep, gotta make him bleed out, only way. Can't have that hanging over my head like some fucking noose, can't keep looking back atcha, wondering when ya'll come calling. Gotta end it, gotta make it go away.*" Jeff reached into his pocket and pulled out the tip of Cliff's nose, then tossed it into the toilet. Cliff thrust forward and the tip of the blade found his Adam's apple. Jeff felt the blade catch the cartilage; it was an obstruction he hadn't anticipated. So he thrust harder, and twisted right. The blade went all the way in, to the top of the wooden handle. The movement felt smoother, so he went with it and pulled the blade that way to continue the trajectory. He used tiny sawing movements as he went to make the effort a little easier. The blood came slowly at first, but as the blade continued through and the tip found the empty space of Cliff's throat, the blood began to pour. He choked on it as it surged into his lungs. Jeff withdrew the blade after it found a tendon. Cliff began uncontrollable spasms. He retched great clots of grey phlegm and dark red.

Ruth, still in agony from the burns to her retinas, didn't have a clue what was happening. She sat in a corner beside the toilet basin and whimpered.

Jeff thrust again, this time a swift stab into Cliff's left eye, then another to the right. *"Yeah that's got it, that's the way, that's gonna do it. No more shit from this asshole, no more second chance for you, you shitbag."* "Excuse me." Jeff pushed Cliff's head to one side so he could reach the handle and flush the toilet.

"Jeff, enough. That's it!" Tears streamed down Glynis's face. She pulled the jacket off him.

Jeff stood there grinning at what he'd done. He dropped the knife, slammed the toilet door shut, and then wedged the chair under the handle. "Holy shit! I'm sorry Glyn, but I had no choice. It was the only way I could see to get us out of this."

She hugged him for a second. "Let's get out of here." She took him by the hand and ran towards the stairs. She grabbed a pair of shoes from a pigeon hole, held a sole to her right sole, nodded once, and then continued up the stairs as Cliff's dying cries from behind the toilet door faded.

They loaded the cart as quickly as they could, then Glynis sat down on her saddle.

"Hold on, one more thing." Jeff ran back into the house, grabbed the diary from the reception desk, and then ran downstairs. There he swiftly tore the pages out and scrunched them into balls. He put them on the floor, under the wooden chairs, in the pigeon holes, and halfway under the toilet door. He produced a Zippo, then set light to as many balls of paper as he could before he was forced back upstairs by the smoke.

He jumped onto his saddle. "Come on let's go!"

They were eight blocks away when Jeff pulled on his brakes with a squeak, then scanned the horizon. The moonlight caught a plume of black smoke.

---

3. Shoes, Spacesuit, and Coat

The National Air and Space Museum had taken a lot of damage from the conflict.

"This isn't good, Glyn," said Jeff.

Glynis patted him on the back. "I'll help you find your spacesuit. Don't worry."

"Come on then. We'll find an open space for you to dance too."

They clambered up the rubble that had once been the entrance steps, then climbed over the twisted doorframes and into the foyer. The Boeing aviation hangar looked like an aircraft graveyard. It was as if aircraft from many different decades had collided to come crashing down. Debris was strewn everywhere. Jeff picked up a visitor's guidebook from the dust.

"Do you know where we're going?" said Glynis.

"Yep." He studied the guidebook. "We've gotta keep going through these wrecks, keep to the left." He glanced up and pointed. "The space stuff's through there. Oh, and if you spot any good clothes on the way, tell me."

"I've been thinking for a while now. Why do you think we survived the first attack, and the others – the adults we've seen – why did they survive too?"

He climbed onto the silver wing of a Dakota DC3, then reached down to her. "Been thinking about that a lot myself, actually."

She took his hands and joined him on the wing. "Well?"

"Not sure, but I'd bet that the aliens allowed a small percentage of people to live on purpose."

"Why? It doesn't make sense."

He continued across the wing, climbed down, and then helped her down. "Makes perfect sense really if you think about it. If they really are so old – the aliens I mean – if they really are then one day they will've experienced all that's left behind. Like a finished dinner. So, they allow a few kids and adults to live, the adults look after the kids – perhaps have kids of their own. Then the kids grow up and have their own kids. The aliens get a fresh supply of experiences after a few hundred years."

"So like waiting for the next course in a restaurant?"

"Could say that."

"So why do *we* get the hits?"

"Maybe that's how the aliens want it – kinda fills us up with life, makes us richer, tastier for when they detonate the next bombs. They probably planted bombs where they knew we'd build cities again. Leave 'em there for a few thousand years, let the experiences build up again, and BOOM!"

Glynis thought for a while. "Do you think they've done that before, here, on the Earth? Like a never-ending banquet for them?"

"Greedy bastards."

"I wish you wouldn't cuss!"

"Come on. We're nearly there."

The display case glass lay in broken shards at their feet. Splinters peppered by dust were unable to reflect the morning sunlight streaming through the tall vacant window frames behind them.

"Which one?" said Glynis.

"Doesn't really matter – as long as they've been in space." Jeff looked along the line of suits and read the plaques beneath them. "That one will do, that's been in space. Give me a hand to drag it into the restaurant area. We'll clear the tables and chairs and have plenty of room for you to dance."

Later, they stood in the middle of the restaurant floor.

"I'm gonna break a rule," said Jeff. "How about you put on the shoes after I've got the top half of the suit on and then hold my hands. See what happens?"

"But you said never share."

"I know, but if my guess is right it's gonna be great!"

Glynis pulled on the shoes and tied the ribbons tightly as Jeff put on the suit. They faced each other and held hands.

It wasn't cold as he had expected it to be. Neither was it silent. A tune filled the vacuum of space as he stared down to the Earth and all its beauty. It was a very long time ago. The music grew, and he noticed her, weightless and free, laughing and pirouetting towards him through space. He laughed back, holding out his hands to catch hers. They danced in orbit now, the pas de deux from Tchaikovsky's *The Sleeping Beauty*. Calmly they carried their steps forward as their orbits began to decay. Faster and faster around the Earth they danced, oblivious at last to their realities, sharing the memories and abilities from what they wore. The music swelled and they laughed, knowing this dance must come to an end all too soon.

They broke hands and she danced away from him, backward through the void as he hung there motionless, watching her. It was time. The shoes were removed and the suit climbed out of.

They stood there looking at each other, both waiting for the other to speak. Finally she picked up her shoes. "Thank you."

He smiled and gave a low bow. "No problem, and thank you."

"Jeff, there were good people, weren't there? Before the bombs?"

"There were. Maybe there still are."

"Will the aliens turn good after seeing the good people's lives – see they've done the wrong thing?"

"I don't know, Glyn. Could be that's what they need in their lives. A balance, to help them bring up their kids, if they have any, to make all of them better aliens. I still don't understand why they let us let off all our bombs and mess up the planet – they could've done that on their own."

"Simple," said Glynis. "So they had the memories of the survivors that died to look forward to. Wandering around the ruins with bits of them hanging off, looking for help, watching their families die in pain. A little seasoning for their feast."

Jeff, looking for clothes along the way, guided them toward an exit on the other side of the building.

"What's that, down there?" Glynis pointed to a large hole in the floor where a huge rocket exhibit had fallen and broken through. "What's it say on the visitor's map?"

"Dunno. Nothing's marked here."

She jumped up and down and tapped his arm. "I bet it's a storeroom! Wonder what we might find down there. Maybe Tutankhamun's mask!"

"That's in Egypt, Glyn. This is an aviation and space museum, but yeah, I know where you're coming from. There *could* be a great stash of stuff down there. The mother lode of historical clothes." He looked around. "Just gotta find a way down."

They pushed a plane wing down into the hole, slid down it, and then climbed over the engine.

The basement was tidy, almost as if someone had been looking after the place since the bombs went off. They wandered down corridors and searched for storeroom doors and the potential trinkets within. At the end of a wide corridor, two giant double doors with "CONTROL" written in large red letters barred the way.

"Control of what?" said Glynis.

"Maybe the generator room for the museum, or where they control all the animated exhibits from."

"Let's find out." She pushed open the doors.

In the darkness, the tiny console lights flickered. Row upon row of desks faced a huge screen with a map of the world laid out in two joined ovals. The ceiling lights came on as Jeff and Glynis entered.

"This has nothing to do with the museum," said Jeff.

"Doesn't look real to me," said Glynis. "Looks like an exhibit. Maybe this is where they build them. Could be one that's not finished – looks like a space control room from one of the old movies."

"No, I don't think so." Jeff walked down the wide centre aisle steps, then extended his arms. "Why would it all still be on?"

Glynis followed him. "They could have been testing it. You know, when the bombs went off?"

"So where are the barriers? What about the plaques explaining everything? This is something more important than an exhibit. I think this is for real."

"A real what?"

As Jeff reached the bottom step he noticed next to the chairs the bones protruding from the bright blue uniforms with crisp white shirts. In front of the screen stood a desk with a skeleton slumped in a big leather chair. It wore a long grey overcoat, black suit, white shirt, and black tie.

"I think I know what this is," said Jeff. On the floor next to the body in the chair was a floral-patterned dress covering bones. Next to that, a long black cloak covered a black suit with a white clerical collar. The arrangement of bones seemed as though the person had fallen to the side whilst kneeling.

Upon the desk was a raised circular emblem above a small control panel with a single recessed button, its clear plastic cover hinged open.

"That's the seal of the President of the United States," said Jeff. "We found the mother lode! This is where the nuke strike was launched from." He pointed to the bones. "That was the President, she was the first lady, and that was probably a priest."

"But why would this place be under the museum?"

"Why not? Where do you expect the control room to be? In the White House? Nah, it's still in Washington but it's out of the way here. Last place you'd expect it to be." He looked around. "There's probably a tunnel leading here from the White House, an underground mini subway or something."

"The coat, in the chair. That's the President's coat, right?"

Before she could say another word, he pulled it from the bones and draped it over his shoulders.

The surge of emotion was incredible. His eyes shut tightly and his body quivered as he bent forward to steady himself upon the desk. All the fear of consequences, of duty, expectation, conflict, and arguments and of what had to be done. All the suffering caused by the push of one little red button, beneath it a simple electrical connection destined to wipe out centuries of history and millions of innocent lives. But along with that came a resolute feeling of righteousness, of unquestionable authority and destiny. He saw the detonations in his head, the blast waves dissipating, measured perfectly so their radiation would overlap just enough at their edges to maximize the effect. The targets had been repeatedly debated: military installations, strategic cities, ports, areas most likely to be the centres of the enemies' regrouping efforts. All agreed upon, casualty lists compiled for maximum effect and efficiency. He'd read them all, and as he lay in bed he wept with the knowledge of what had to be done, perhaps, one day. But upon this final day not one shred of emotion was allowed to penetrate the hardened shell he'd struggled so hard to maintain around him. There would be no show of guilt. All eyes were upon him now, all knew what he had to do, but did he have the strength when it came down to it? Of course, there was no other choice. After all, it was a simple task, pushing a button.

For Jeff it became too much. He wept as he bent over the desk.

Glynis pulled the Armageddon coat from his shoulders. As it briefly touched both of them she saw a vision, a future where they were adults bound as one, spliced together in one body. He was reaching out with blood on his hand as she tried to hold him back. Their body was bruised and diseased, decaying from the constant hits they'd experienced from the clothes. It was a possible future she realised, and as she dropped the coat to the floor the image vanished.

His breathing was hard, and he tried to speak, to thank her, but this experience was too overpowering. He looked upward and gulped in the recycled air until his heart began to relax. Finally, wiping his tears, he turned to her. "Too much Glyn, far too much. Don't try it. It's not worth it."

"You gonna be okay?" Glynis knew he had not yet seen the vision she had.

He nodded. "Just give me a few minutes. We're leaving that one there." He pointed to the Armageddon coat. "Never, ever again. Never."

As Jeff tried to extinguish the images circling around his head, he felt something over his shoulders. At once the images began to fade and as the garment touched them both, her vision of their combined bodies vanished.

Glynis stepped away. The clerical cloak draped over Jeff slowly erased the guilt, the omnipotence, the righteousness. It spoke to him in a reassuring tone.

Once the Armageddon coat's memories vanished, he felt the threads of anger and hatred unravel, then flutter away. One by one his synapses were purged, blessed, and forgiven by the purity contained in the cloak. Away with the violence, away with the blood on his hands – their hands, the lives of so many men and women cemented into his soul and all their remembered lives. Their greed vanished and he was full and without need, their envy dissolved and he was satisfied, their unjust hatred of their brothers purged and he felt only love. His breathing relaxed and he finally stood up straight, then removed the cloak.

"Thank you Glyn. I feel so different. Almost every memory the garments have given me, the adults' experiences, nearly all gone now." He carefully folded the cloak, then placed it upon the desk over the Presidential Seal. "It's the most precious garment we could ever find, if you think about it."

She nodded and placed her hands on her hips. "You're thinking what *I'm* thinking?"

He tilted his head and mimicked her. "What *am* I thinking?"

"You're thinking that every now and then we drape that thing around our shoulders and erase every hit we've had, so we can have them all fresh, all over again, so it's like we've never had them. Like tasting Pepsi for the first time. That fizzy tingle that goes up your nose and makes you sneeze?"

He held out his palm for a high-five and she jumped up and slapped it. "You've got it Glyn. It's a fucking detox cloak."

She picked up the Armageddon coat, then threw it to him. "I keep telling you, *don't cuss*!"

Howard Watts *is a writer, artist and composer living in Seaford. He also provides the wraparound cover art for this issue. His artwork can be seen in its native resolution on his DeviantArt page: hswatts.deviantart.com. His novel*
The Master of Clouds is available on Kindle.

Scrotal Quilt

Douglas J. Ogurek

Gick was stitching the next sac onto her scrotal quilt when a "gol-gol-gol" sound came from the nearby forest. The space explorer on the ground screamed and clutched his bleeding crotch. Gick had just chopped off the spaceman's "modules" after spraying furniture polish into his helmet, tossing in a match, and then closing the face shield.

The space explorer opened the shield. Smoke billowed out. "Gahhhk."

"No. Gick."

"What did you... you're a... gahhhk."

Gick raised her hands and squeaked.

Her fairy audience started glowing.

The "gol-gol-gol" grew louder.

The space explorer roared, "You should be teaching, teaching the little kiddies."

Gick rubbed his "modules" on her pink onesie. "Today's lesson is in asssstrology."

"You should be a mommy."

"Exploring Uranus? That takes balls." She shoved the testicles up the space explorer's "aft fuselage".

Gick sewed the space explorer's sac onto the quilt, then showed the fairies the nearly finished product, which was commissioned by the Museum of Unconventional Femmes Fatales (aka MUFF). Just three more sacs to go.

The "gol-gol-gol" sounded again, but the fairies' cheer of "gorsake gorsake gorsake" overpowered it.

They glowed brighter and lifted Gick to the treetops, where she raised her fist. "Yeahyeahyeahyeah goo. Fuck yeah."

Beyond the forest, green and blue splotches marked a cliff face. The splotches came from the bird known as the pooflinger.

While she was up there, Gick also saw a man on the path between the forest and the mountain. He carried a long pole with a blade attached to the top.

The sky turned overcast and Gick used some of the space explorer's veins to tie pigtails. Her next benefactor, a vampire, appeared.

Gick went to her cart of ultra-effeminate items, then offered the vampire a cupcake. It had pink frosting and a red heart. The vampire used his staff to knock the cupcake out of her hand. He held his cell phone against her arm. It beeped. "A match. I will drink your blood, Object. Your blood."

"The repetition, the rep-e-ti-tion, makes it more dramatic."

"It's a vamp app, a vamp app that reveals your doom."

Gick picked up the cupcake, then rubbed the pink frosting all over her face. "Doof."

Again the sound came from the forest. This time, the "gol-gol-gol" was followed by a "mee-ning-ning." There was a sadness in it.

The vampire chuckled and caressed the shiny teal that topped his staff. "Such a heart-rending call. Perhaps it's mourning you already."

Gick, her face covered in pink, took from her cart a busty doll with a floral-patterned dress. "This is Joannie Joyjugs, a doll. And I am Gick, a person."

The fairies buzzed, but the vampire played goth music on his phone, hissed, and lunged at them.

Gick clawed her frosting-covered hands before the vampire. "Arrrgh."

"I see your behaviour is as mature as your wardrobe."

The "mee-ning" stretched from the forest. The vampire showed his fangs and tapped the polished teal. Gick had noticed that same colour embedded in the space explorer's sleeve... just before she dumped boiling water on him.

Gick spoke into a walkie-talkie. "MUFF curator, calling MUFF curator."

A woman's voice came through. "Ah ha ha. Rumple*tilt*skin... ha!"

Gick slid her onesie slipper against the ground. "The vampire is dashing. He is sophisticated. He is elegant."

The curator said, "The Evil *Schlep*mother. Ha! I like ribbons!"

Gick took from her cart of ultra-effeminate items a stick with a long ribbon attached to it. She used it to do a rhythmic gymnastics routine.

The vampire hissed and reached toward her.

Gick wrapped the ribbon around him, then pulled.

The vampire squirmed and tried to look at his phone, but the ribbon was too tight.

Gick pulled tighter. "This ribbon stores solar energy, courtesy of my sun."

The vampire started to smoke. "Release me. Bitch."

"Hey." Gick put a hand on her hip and pointed toward the cloud-covered sun. "That makes *you* a sun of a bitch."

The sun pulled apart the clouds, showed two burning cheeks, and then covered itself back up.

"Doof. Mooned by the sun."

The seared vampire bore his fangs, but Gick held up Joannie Joyjugs. Spikes broke through the doll's dress where the nipples would be. "I filled these in a baptismal font. How 'bout a 'nip' of holy water?" Gick shoved the spikes into the vampire's eyes.

The vampire made a percolating noise and fell.

"I know... you can't keep your eyes off her." Gick used a pliers to pull out his fangs. She shoved one up his pee hole. "Here's a new-*fang*led look."

The vampire, with Joannie Joyjugs still stuck to his face, gurgled and swung his staff. "Object, you..."

Gick grabbed the staff, then broke it over her knee. "Staff meeting at six o'clock sharp." She repeatedly shoved the sharp end into the vampire's "coffin".

Then Gick chopped off his "fledglings". She put the heart from the cupcake on his "shadow stick". "Look. He's got a heart on." Then she cut that off. She speared the testicles on the staff, then topped it with the penis. "Looks like you have a staff infection."

The fairies brightened and started their "gorsake" chant.

Gick tucked the vampire's sac into the doll's dress like a bib. Then she held the genital shish kebab before the doll. "Come on now Joannie. Better eat your weenies. And these have nuts."

As Gick sewed the vampire's sac onto her quilt – two left! – the desperate "meee-ning" sounded again, but the fairies overwhelmed it with their "gorsake gorsake."

They lifted Gick and she shouted, "Yuh yuh yuh ya-hah cocka." When she was elevated, Gick again saw the man with the long, bladed pole. He wore a satchel, and studied the treetops. Farther back, a pooflinger flew by and hurled its poop. A red splotch exploded on the cliff face.

Gick's next benefactor, a wizard, gripped his crotch and thrust his hips. "Rumph rumph bumph."

Gick took from her cart of ultra-effeminate items a pink castle. "Let's play some mystical shit!"

The wizard extended his hand – his ring had that

same teal colour – and the castle floated toward him. The "gol-gol-gol" sounded closer.

Gick put on a tiara, grabbed a star-topped wand, and then promenaded toward the wizard.

The wizard's erection pushed out his robe. He sat, then slapped his lap. "Mmm. Mmm. Wench, sit on my lap."

Gick tossed a fistful of muck straight up. "This is what's inside a vampire." It slapped onto her head.

The pink castle broke apart mid-air, then crashed to the ground. The wizard lifted his cloak to reveal his erect "wand". "Bumph rumph take that off, barmaid."

Intestinal slop covered Gick's face and onesie. So did blood. She spoke into the walkie-talkie. "We have a casticular guest."

The MUFF curator belched and a cloud came out of the walkie-talkie. "This one, Headless *Horns*man. Ha! This one. I like palaces."

The wizard rubbed the teal-topped ring along his member and chuckled when the cloud reached him. "This smells of laudanum."

"Ha!" said the curator. "Queen of *Farts*."

"My wand's stronger than yours." Gick slashed her wand. Its star severed his "wizardhood". He bellowed and fell back. She turned him over, then lifted his cloak. He was "commando" – maybe "sorcerer" is a better word. "Madam Curator, I can't give you a palace, but how about a 'pale ass'?"

Gick spotted the source of the "gol-gol-gol". It was a pooflinger perched in a tree at the forest's edge. Typically, the birds kept silent, but this one seemed troubled.

The walkie-talkie crackled. "I like conjure."

"Presto chango." Gick farted in the wizard's face. "I just cast a smell."

The fairies chanted enthusiastically.

The wizard picked up his member and moaned. "You should be serving me ale. Wench."

"Aye, great soothsayer. I have a heaping portion of ail coming up." Gick picked up a turret and a drawbridge from the broken pink castle.

"Witch."

"I was thinking the same thing. Which?" Gick raised the turret. "YOU... SHALL NOT... GAS!" Up it went into the wizard's "secret chamber."

The distressed pooflinger dropped to the ground, then hopped around and released a tortured "meee-ning". Gick watched it, but the fairies glowed and "gorsaked" exuberantly.

The MUFF curator said, "I like moats. Ha!"

Gick placed the wizard's "cauldron" in the toy castle's entry, then repeatedly slammed the drawbridge against it until his "jewels" spilled out. Then she impaled the testicles on the points of her tiara. "Like my new ball cap?"

The wizard grabbed his chest and his teal ring glimmered. "Guh. Guh. Uhhhguh."

"Geh. Geh. Geh." Gick peed on the wizard's face. The stream ripped off his skin. "I may not be a wizard, but I sure can 'whiz hard.'"

She sewed the wizard's sac onto her quilt. One more to go!

The MUFF curator said, "Our greatest artist."

The fairies squeezed their nipples and glowing nectar flowed out. They lifted Gick, who shouted "Uga-uga-uga-muhcunt." She saw three pooflinger receptacles hanging in the treetops. The birds could only make the teardrop-shaped receptacles during their first year. They hung them from the branches and used them to hold their colourful, mate-attracting poo. One of the receptacles, she noticed, was sliced open.

The fairies lifted Gick higher and higher. The man

with the bladed pole placed something orange in his satchel.

The potential final contributor to Gick's quilt wore a suit and sunglasses. He did not wear socks. Chic.

Gick extended a pink cupcake. "Yoof doof."

"Those are a bit Petunia Berryfrost for my tastes. Petunia Berryfrost... I just made that up." He tugged one of Gick's pigtails and chuckled. "One doesn't get my body by eating cupcakes, but how about a fuckcake? Yeeoo!"

"How about a bluckshmake?" Gick clapped and smashed the cupcake.

He touched Gick's nose. "Shouldn't you be wearing some makeup for me?"

"Let's break the eyes." Gick hopped over to the moaning wizard, then shoved her tiara's points into his eyes. He whimpered. She rubbed his vitreous (i.e. eye goop) on her face for a nice lustre, slit his throat, and then rubbed his blood onto her cheeks. "Isn't it magikill?"

The troubled pooflinger, still on the ground, looked into the trees. "Gol-gol-gol."

The man danced seductively. His cufflinks gleamed with the same teal that Gick saw on the space explorer, the vampire, and the wizard. "Do what I say. I'll save you. I'll fuck you."

Gick handed him a bag of dirt. "I like dirt."

"Dirt is so... dirty."

"Dirt grows stuff."

"You should be clean. A trophy. Do what I say." He hurled the bag into the forest.

Gick raised her hands and squeaked. "Hey, that's my dirtbag." Some of the wizard's eye goop fell on her onesie.

The man pulled out a paddle. "You'll go shopping,

I'll go to work. Then I'll come home and spank you and fuck you. Yeeoo!"

Gick put on false eyelashes that extended two feet.

The pooflinger flew into the tree, then perched beside the split receptacle.

"I have no weaknesses." The man took off his suit to reveal a superhero outfit. A teal orb glowed at its centre.

Gick hopped to her cart of ultra-effeminate items. She selected two pink plastic teacups, then handed one to him.

The superhero smashed his teacup. He pointed at the orb. "You like this look. It uses real pooflinger waste. Extremely rare. Extremely valuable."

Gick realized that the man she'd seen earlier had been using the bladed pole to slice open pooflinger receptacles hanging from the trees, then steal the vibrant dung stored within them.

The walkie-talkie crackled and the MUFF curator came on. "Guh... shick-a... guh."

Gick curtsied and her super lashes gleamed. "This debonair man, this Adonis, trying to sweep me off my feet."

The pooflinger pecked at the split in its receptacle. With nothing to store its poop, the bird would never be able to fling it at the right time to attract a lifelong mate.

A fart came through the walkie-talkie. "Ah! The key of *Poo*beard."

The superhero cringed and waved his paddle before his face. "Dirty. Heinous." He grabbed Gick's wrist, then brought her hand around her back. "I'll have no weaknesses. I'll take you to the clothing store and play Stacey Lacebottom music. Stacey Lacebottom... I made that up. You'll try on different outfits and look sexy. Do what I say. And I'll laugh and look amazed."

Gick cut a hole in the crotch of her onesie, then

held her pink teacup beneath her. Glop plopped into it.

The superhero put his sunglasses on the eyeless wizard, who responded, "Ahhhhk." Then the superhero danced and his teal orb gleamed. Spikes came out of his paddle. "Yeeoo! I'll take you out back to the woodshed."

The pooflinger in the tree pooped, then put its bright orange faeces – each bird had uniquely coloured poo – in its receptacle. The faeces slipped through the gap and the bird wailed, "Meeee-ning... meeee-ning-ning-ning."

The curator made a hacking noise. "Gick, our most revered artist. I like ghouls and *cob*lins."

Gick mixed hot sauce with her secretions in the pink teacup. "Tealtime." She tossed it into the superhero's face.

He screamed and clutched his eyes.

"Naughty boy. You deserve a lashing." Gick batted her two-foot-long eyelashes and the tiny razors on their ends scratched his corneas.

He fell to the ground, then reached toward the sky. "You'll take care of the kids and go out and buy purses and expensive coffee. Yee... oo."

"Pee poo." Gick cut open the superhero's leggings, tore off his two "sidekicks", and then stuck his teal cufflinks in them. "I just gave you blue balls."

"You can be a superhero," he said, "but you must be sexy." Then he pooped himself.

The MUFF curator laughed. "Ha! *Poop*erman."

The pooflinger "gol-gol-goled" and its orange poop sat on the forest floor, unseen by potential mates.

Gick grabbed the superhero's "superpole". "Well, there's no woodshed, but I can sure shed wood." Then she sliced it off.

The superhero screamed. "I'll come home and you'll

make dinner and change diapers. And you'll dance for me. Like Susie Screwmewill. I made... that..."

Gick stretched his sac over her mouth, then batted her sharp eyelashes and belly danced. Then she stuffed his member into his mouth. "Susie Screwyou*wont*."

The superhero groaned and touched his teal orb. "I. Am. More. Powerful."

Gick ripped out the teal orb, then repeatedly slammed it into his bleeding crotch. "Look. A cock-a-teal." She grabbed the spiked paddle, then rolled him over so we was on his hands and knees. "Doggie paddle." She spanked him repeatedly. And pointedly.

Gick finished the quilt, then held it up. "Yeahyeahyeahyeah goo. Fuck yeah."

The pooflinger with the destroyed receptacle released the loudest and longest "meeee-ning" yet.

The fairies ejaculated floral-scented glitter.

"Gick, the *Gick*ed Witch." The MUFF curator hacked joyously. "Bring in the scrotal quilt for the exhibit!"

Gick turned off the walkie-talkie.

The fairies chanted "gorsake gorsake" and lifted Gick up up up... all the way up to the ruined pooflinger receptacle. She took it down, shaped the scrotal quilt into a new receptacle, and then hung it.

Later, the pooflinger inserted its orange faeces, and the new receptacle held.

Douglas J. Ogurek*'s fiction, though banned on Mars, appears in over 40 Earth publications. Ogurek founded the literary subgenre known as unsplatterpunk, which uses splatterpunk conventions (e.g. extreme violence, gore, taboo subject matter) to deliver a positive message. Ogurek also reviews films for Theaker's Quarterly Fiction. More at www.douglasjogurek.weebly.com.*

The Quarterly Review

Reviews by Rafe McGregor, Douglas J. Ogurek and Rose M. Rye

Douglas J. Ogurek's work has appeared in the BFS Journal, The Literary Review, Morpheus Tales, Gone Lawn, and several anthologies. Douglas's website can be found at www.douglasjogurek.weebly.com.

Rafe McGregor Rafe McGregor is the author of The Value of Literature, The Architect of Murder, six collections of short fiction, and one hundred and fifty magazine articles, journal papers, and review essays. He lectures at the University of York and can be found online at @rafemcgregor.

Rose M. Rye is an actual woman, honestly, but she's writing for us under a pseudonym because she doesn't really want to be hassled at work by people who disagree with her opinions about television.

*We don't have a policy on ratings, other than
that reviewers use them or not as they prefer!*

Books

Autumn Snow 1: The Pit of Darkness, by Martin Charbonneau, Joe Dever and Gary Chalk (Megara Entertainment)

Stephen Theaker has been kind enough to allow me to
indulge my nostalgia for 1980s fantasy gamebooks in
his magazine and over the course of three reviews –
The Voyage of the Moonstone (TQF55), *The Buccaneers
of Shadaki*, and *The Storms of Chai* (both TQF57) –
I've charted the remarkable story of Joe Dever's Lone
Wolf series. The latest of my reports contains a couple
of surprises of the kind I've come to expect by now,
given the series' incredibly complicated publishing
history, characterised by first falling victim to and then
being perpetuated by the domination of internet
technology at the turn of the century. To begin at the
beginning, I first found out about *The Pit of Darkness*
courtesy of Project Aon (www.projectaon.org), the
voluntary organisation that has done so much to keep
the series alive during its many years in the publishing
wilderness, in a bulletin listing the current availability
of Lone Wolf products dated 8 July 2016. Megara
Entertainment founder Mikaël Louys began
crowdfunding for the volume in September 2014, the
main purpose of which was to secure the services of
the original Lone Wolf illustrator, Gary Chalk, who
had an apparently acrimonious split with Dever
between the release of *Castle Death* (#7, 1986) and *The
Jungle of Horrors* (#8, 1987). The gamebook is only
available from the Megara website direct
(www.megara-entertainment.com) and has been

released in both French and English versions. The two
are presented distinctly on the website and although

the price is quite steep (about £30 at the time of my purchase, no doubt more now), it includes postage and packaging and my copy arrived promptly and in perfect condition. I nonetheless have two small complaints about Megara. First, they don't seem to advertise very well – I ordered immediately after following the link from Project Aon and the copy I received is already a "THIRD PRINTING, REVISED" – what happened to the first two printings? Second, and this may well be the reason for being in a third printing already (assuming all three were released in 2016), there are quite a few typos and formatting errors in the book (albeit all minor).

The volume itself is entirely pleasing, if printed in a slightly unusual format (a hardback that is either medium octavo in size or extremely close to it) with a wonderful colour cover by Chalk, around double the ten full-page black-and-white illustrations originally intended, and large easy-to-read print. Chalk's artwork is highly stylised and his clear lines, imaginative use of negative space, and slightly disproportionate figures will be instantly recognisable to his fans from the eighties. His style is especially well-suited to children's illustrations, in which market he has worked extensively, although I noted that the innocence and simplicity of his original Lone Wolf work has been eclipsed by a vision of Magnamund (the world of Lone Wolf) that is both more sinister and more intricately detailed. Chalk's Vassagonian pirates are a perfect example, depicted in all their bloodthirsty savagery on the pages adjacent to sections 7 and 256 – not a *Pirates-of-the-Caribbean*-style comedy character in sight. *The Pit of Darkness* thus has two major selling points: it is the first Lone Wolf gamebook to unite Dever and Chalk in thirty years (Dever is credited as having "Edited and Augmented" the volume) and it is the first Lone Wolf gamebook to feature a female protagonist. The latter is particularly welcome, although in fairness to Dever the eighties wasn't exactly a decade known for its equality of opportunity. Nor has the Kai Order eschewed gender discrimination entirely as male and female candidates are required to pursue different paths, the former to become New Order Kai Lords and the latter to become New Order Kai Konor. Autumn Snow is one of the latter, having joined the Konor when she was seven, mastered five of the ten Kai disciplines over the next seven years, and reached the rank of Initiate. The Lords and Konor study the same disciplines and this level of expertise puts Autumn Snow at precisely the same level as Lone Wolf at the beginning of the series, in *Flight from the Dark* (#1, 1984).

There is no explicit dating, but the story is set a year after *Dawn of the Dragons* (#18, 1992), presumably in MS 5081, while Lone Wolf is away, presumably on his last mission as a player character, *The Curse of Naar* (#20, 1993). This is a post-Darklords Magnamund, but is – just like our own post-Cold War world in the nineties – going through more than a few teething troubles. Autumn Snow is invited to join her principal instructor, Kai Lord Silver Flame, on what appears to be a routine investigation of sightings of former Darklands creatures on the Isle of Kirlu, which is part of the Kirlundian archipelago off the coast of Sommerlund. The first part of the gamebook takes place at sea, before Kirlu is reached, as the merchant ship on which Autumn Snow and Silver Flame are travelling is attacked by the aforementioned bloodthirsty savages. The battle involves a series of tough and exciting combats and leaves Autumn Snow the sole survivor of the crew, with Silver Flame missing in action presumed dead. Despite the fatal encounter with the pirates there is still a chance that the main mission is routine, but of course it proves not to be and when Autumn Snow arrives in Misty Bay after a dangerous journey on foot, she learns that Giaks (Magnamund's orcs) have been sighted in the ruins of Wytch Aieta Nematah's citadel. Autumn Snow infiltrates the ruins, finds a lot more than Giaks to fight, and the final part of the gamebook switches from a wilderness to a dungeon adventure (to use the old Dungeons & Dragons terminology). The Pit of the title lies beneath the ruins and it quickly becomes evident that the appearance of the Vassagonian pirates was no accident as the Vassagonians and Drakkarim, two of Magnamund's most evil human races, are in league together.

From a gaming point of view, I thought the level of difficulty was particularly well-pitched, the mission challenging rather than suicidal. The toughest combat is probably with the Pit itself and players will need one of the disciplines of Mindblast, Mindshield, or a high initial Combat Skill to survive. With regard to disciplines, I found Tracking useful and – as always – Weaponskill and Healing, although Martin Charbonneau has introduced his own take on the latter. With regard to the actual mechanics of play (which follows the Lone Wolf gamebooks exactly and also has the traditional 350 sections), I was very interested to see that a third option is being tried for the Healing discipline. Back when I first came to the series in the mid-eighties Healing allowed one point of Endurance to be restored for each section where one was not involved in combat. When I chose my five disciplines, Healing was my first choice, followed by Weaponskill (the former to restore my character's Endurance, the latter to boost his Combat Skill) and I can't imagine how anyone could have managed without both. Dever must have decided that Healing was too powerful – and, in retrospect, with the Sommerswerd, Healing, and a bit of commonsense I don't think there was too much to challenge Lone Wolf post-Darklords – because in *The Voyage of the Moonstone* (#21, 1994), which launched the New Order series, a limit was placed on the amount of Endurance the discipline could be used to restore. In *The Pit of Darkness*, the limit is gone and Endurance is restored at the rate of two points rather than one, but only at selected sections (indicated by a grey rather than black section number). There are naturally never any grey sections around when you need them, but allowing for the fact that I've only used this system in a single gameplay I think it is the best so far and part of the reason for the balance I noted – not too easy, like the Kai Grand Master series (books 13 to 20), or too hard, like the tail end of the New Order series (books 21 to 32). Having discovered the secret of the Pit, the adventure ends with Autumn Snow *en route* to the Maakenmire, a swamp south of the Wildlands. The second Autumn Snow adventure is *Slaves of the Mire*, but there are no publication details available in *The Pit of Darkness* or on the Megara website. My worry as I write this is that it will have to be crowdfunded too, in which case we're unlikely to see it in print for two years (given the rate at which *The Pit of Darkness* was printed). Hopefully, that's not the case, especially if the series is reaching new fans with Dever completing the long-awaited final four New Order adventures. I think the Autumn Snow series could be an outstanding addition to Magnamund – the best since the Magnakai series ended with *The Masters of Darkness* (#12, 1988) – but word will need to spread beyond the Megara website if it is to reach its potential. *Rafe McGregor*

The Monarch of the Glen, by Neil Gaiman and Daniel Egnéus (Headline)

Neil Gaiman's *American Gods* was first published in 2001 and then re-published in an expanded tenth anniversary edition. Remarkably, the latter – which has been available as a delightfully captivating audiobook since 2012 – is a literal "author's cut", i.e. Gaiman's original novel, published without the considerable editorial redactions of the published version and therefore substantially longer (such are the perks of fame). I thought *American Gods* was deserving of its critical and popular success although I was disappointed that Gaiman hadn't integrated the monotheistic religions into his universe, a strategy which was obviously expedient, but felt inconsistent. The audiobook (but not the tenth anniversary edition) contains a deleted passage in which Shadow meets Christ, offering a tantalising taste of how Gaiman might have treated the monotheistic gods (oxymoron intended), but the encounter raises more questions than it answers. As an aside on adaptations, the television series of *American Gods* is due for release by Fremantle Media on an unspecified date in 2017. Despite *The Monarch of the Glen* being marketed by Amazon as part of the "American Gods Novella" series, there is no mention of any such series from publisher Headline on or in the book itself. The narrative is indeed set in the world of *American Gods* and even shares the same protagonist in Shadow, but is also – as one might expect from a storyteller of Gaiman's skill – perfectly self-contained and can be enjoyed without having read the novel.

The novella (or perhaps short story, it's difficult to tell with all the illustrations) was first published in *Legends II*, a collection of speculative fiction edited by Robert Silverberg, in 2003. This version has been coreleased with *American Gods* and *Anansi Boys* (first published in 2005), which is also set in the *American Gods* universe, as well as the other "American Gods Novella", *Black Dog*, also reviewed in this issue. All four volumes are illustrated by Daniel Egnéus, who cites his influences as Arthur Rackham and Gustave

Doré. He certainly displays the former's flair for line and the latter's ability to represent the otherworldly and there is also a strong surrealist sense of the fluidity of shape, reality, and reason in his depictions. The interior illustrations are black and white and they fully capture the darkness of both Gaiman's setting and the subject matter of the tale that unfolds in that setting. Egnéus leaves readers in no doubt that Shadow has arrived in a vital, visceral, and volatile place where the trappings of modernity conceal an ancient and unchanged way of life. Egnéus' work enriches rather than embellishes Gaiman's and my one complaint is that a couple of the titles that form part of the drawings are spoilers and detract from one's intellectual and imaginative engagement in the first instance and from the drama of the fully-realised *dénouement* in the second.

The narrative takes place in the north-west of the Scottish Highlands and is set two years after the conclusion of *American Gods*. Shadow, who may or may not be an incarnation of Baldr (or Baldur or Balder), who may or may not be a god, has spent the interim backpacking across Europe and North Africa and finds himself in an unnamed village somewhere between Thurso and Cape Wrath. The plot begins when, in quick succession, he is offered a weekend job as a bouncer at a local country house and meets an unconventional barmaid named Jennie who regales him with stories of the local lore, particularly those pertaining to the strong Norse influence in what is usually assumed to be a hyper-Celtic culture. The suspense is generated first by the mysterious party, then by its mysterious guests, and finally by the real reason for Shadow's employment. Having uncharitably criticised Egnéus for a couple of slight spoilers, I shall be careful to avoid the same charge myself in raising my quibble with Gaiman. I am also aware how minor this point is in a work that has – words and images combined – provided me with an exceptionally rewarding reading experience and that I shall have complained that it is too revealing and too opaque, which doesn't seem very convincing at all. The opacity is in the title. *The Monarch of the Glen* (1851) is a painting of a red deer stag by Edwin Landseer and has become one of the exemplary and archetypal images of the Highlands specifically and Scotland more generally. Landseer was famous for contributing to the Victorian image of an idyllic Scotland that never existed and for representing anthropomorphic animals in savage struggles for survival against one another, man, and nature. The painting itself – or rather, Landseer's copy of his own painting – appears in the story, the property of Mr Alice, who is hosting the party. Its significance – and given the title, it must surely be significant – is never explained or even suggested and the only commentary is Alice on its popularity and Shadow's silent appraisal of the stag as "haughty, and superior".

My understanding of the painting's significance in the novella is that the shared title is a reference to Shadow, who has been hired to take part in a struggle even more savage than those portrayed by Landseer. In this struggle, Shadow is the symbol of both man against monster and Scotland against its (Norse) invaders. But, just like the criticism that Landseer created a false image of Scotland, Shadow is being set up as a false symbol, one that has no basis in reality. He is, like the English Landseer in the Highlands, a foreigner, and also, as the opening dialogue of the narrative reminds readers, a monster himself – not quite a man and not quite a god. And of course Gaiman is far too sophisticated a writer to allow the simple dichotomies of man/monster, Celtic/Norse, and the relation between them to remain unchallenged. The result is that the explosive climax at the country house does not turn out as expected for any of the participants and Shadow is measured against his own judgement of Landseer's stag. Shadow survives (no spoiler, as he will reappear in *Black Dog*) and the tale concludes with him on a train, heading south with the ultimate aim of bringing his wandering to an end in Chicago. The complexity of the title, the symbolism, and Shadow's character are wonderfully intriguing and if I didn't find the confirmation I was looking for, that may well be because my interpretation is mistaken. I shall, however, make no mistake here: this is a great novella, atmospheric and thrilling, intellectual and unpredictable. *Rafe McGregor*

Black Dog, by Neil Gaiman and Daniel Egnéus (Headline)

Black Dog is one of Neil Gaiman's four *American Gods* stories, all of which have been re-released by Headline in hardback editions illustrated by Daniel Egnéus. The other three are: *American Gods* itself (first published in 2001 and re-released in an expanded tenth anniversary edition in 2011), *The Monarch of the Glen* (also reviewed in this issue), and *Anansi Boys* (first published in 2005). As an update to my previous review, the television adaptation of *American Gods* is due for release as a STARZ original series in 2017, possibly over Easter. Ricky Whittle will play the part of Shadow, Ian McShane the part of Wednesday, and the duo will be joined by a host of familiar faces from the big and small screen. *Black Dog* is a novella (or short story – it is, once again, difficult to tell due to the copious illustrations) and was first published in *Trigger Warning: Short Fictions and Disturbances* (2015), Gaiman's fourth collection of short fiction (excluding his writing for children). The narrative shares the same protagonist with *American Gods*, Shadow, and the temporal setting is easily established: three years after his wife's death and either several weeks or a few months after *The Monarch of Glen*. The latter novella ended with Shadow leaving Scotland by train, his eventual destination Chicago, but

somewhere along the line he exchanged rail for foot and the spatial setting is the first mystery Gaiman presents to his readers. Many clues are provided, some tantalising, some contradictory: the blurb labels a "rural northern village"; but it is not too remote from London; it might be near Glossop; it is surrounded by hills and valleys; it features plenty of drystone walls; and it has its own ghost dog, called Black Shuck. Black Shuck is the name of East Anglia's version of the old English legend, but East Anglia is notoriously flat and I think the name "The Gateway to Hell" is decisive, suggesting Eldon Hole in the Peak Forest and the Peak District (also known as the Derbyshire Dales) more generally. This relocation of Black Shuck to one of the few regions of England that does not have its own ghost dog is the first indication of the categorical originality of Gaiman's re-invention of the legend.

The novella opens with a play on words: the first chapter is titled "The Bar Guest" and *the barghest* is the name of the Yorkshire incarnation of the black dog. Gaiman very quickly provides a series of reflections on and allusions to many of the linguistic and conceptual associations with dogs that are such a prominent part of English culture: the love of dogs as pets, the eternal conflict between cats and dogs and consequent division of human beings into "cat-people" and "dog-people", "black dog" as a description of depression (made famous by Winston Churchill), "black dog" as a favoured name for brands of ale, and the curiosity of a ghost dog that portends or causes death without possessing any corporeality. As the tale develops, he adds the conceptions of prehistoric dire wolves, Odin's wolves (although Odin's nemesis Fenrir seems more appropriate), and the myth of the Wild Hunt. There are also explicit references to Conan Doyle's *The Hound of the Baskervilles* (1902) and, in my opinion, implicit references to Stephen Booth's

Cooper and Fry crime series, which is set in the Peak District and was initiated with the novel *Black Dog* (2001). The combination of these references also serves as a clue that this is as much a mystery as it is a work of speculative fiction. When compared to *The Monarch of the Glen*, Daniel Egnéus' artwork reflects both the change in emphasis from fantasy to mystery and the more hospitable countryside in which Shadow finds himself, where an evening on a hilltop is an experience to be enjoyed rather than a death sentence – or *should* be. Egnéus' drawings are much less visceral than those in *The Monarch of the Glen* and with a few exceptions evoke wonder rather than fear while nonetheless retaining a haunting quality. Like the dog itself, they are shady, shapeshifting, and surreal.

The story starts with Shadow in a public house, where there is much spooky talk of big black dogs and cats walled up in buildings. The village has no accommodation available and a local couple, Ollie and Moira, offer him a room for the night. As the three of them walk home, Ollie thinks he sees Black Shuck and falls into a narcoleptic state. This introduces the natural dimension of Gaiman's take on the black dog, as a manifestation of depression, which grounds the narrative in reality: depressed people recognise their own despair, exemplified by the ghost dog, and either try to kill themselves or simply lose the will to live. Following this motif, Ollie self-harms as soon as he emerges from his semi-consciousness, setting the scene for Shadow remaining in the village for a few days to help Moira look after him. Whether or not I am correct in identifying *Black Dog* as equal parts speculative fiction and mystery, it is certainly focused on a contemporary crime rather than an ancient evil. What raises Gaiman's contribution to the black dog legend from the original to the exceptional is the way he not only offers a rationalisation of its continued existence, but binds the supernatural explanation to its own special logic. The ghosts that inhabit this particular piece of the *American Gods* universe are not restricted to the canine variety and the relationship between the villain and the ghost dog and between Shadow and the benevolent ghost is explained by the metaphor of flame and moth. Human beings, warm with their life blood coursing through them, are the flames that attract the attention of moth-like ghosts, which clarifies the reciprocal relation between corporeal and non-corporeal: the moth flying too close to the flame can either extinguish that flame or be destroyed by it. *Rafe McGregor*

Films

Arrival, by Eric Heisserer (21 Laps et al.)

The lingo of time: UFO film touches down as one of year's most impressive cinematic offerings.

I didn't think that any film last year would stack up to *10 Cloverfield Lane*. So much for that. *Arrival* offers another strong female lead in an equally gripping sci-fi masterpiece.

The latter film, directed by Denis Villeneuve, in many ways transcends its genre to become, in this reviewer's opinion, an Oscar contender. Inherent in the title is the film's big idea. This isn't an *Independence Day* or *War of the Worlds* alien invasion action film. It's merely an *arrival* of extraterrestrial vessels, and protagonist Dr. Louise Banks (Amy Adams) must decode the aliens' language.

Skilful in its audio and visual manoeuvrings, *Arrival* plays with our perceptions of language and time, and challenges our tech-driven migration toward impulsive behaviour. The film leaves the patient viewer processing its implications long after the credits roll. It even gets into Tennyson's "Tis better to have loved and lost" bit.

Adams, along with supporting cast Jeremy Renner and Forest Whitaker, offers a strong performance. All three actors let the film's innovative premise and

underlying mystery, rather than their characters, take centre stage.

The opening scene reveals that Dr Banks experiences a major loss. At the university where she teaches linguistics, she discovers that twelve alien craft have touched down at various points across the Earth. Colonel Weber (Whitaker) recruits Banks (the language expert) and theoretical physicist Dr Ian Donnelly (Renner, the scientist), then brings them to the Montana field over which the North American alien contingent hovers. Weber wants the duo to get into the ship and figure out why the visitors are here and what they want. This objective drives the remainder of the film, which builds to a Shyamalan-like climax that packs an emotional wallop.

Strong Connection with the Protagonist
The filmmakers' tight focus on Banks keeps the viewer in tune with her feelings. One example is her reaction to the news of the arrival. She (and we) learn of the event not by seeing giant spaceships approaching, but rather via a news report in her quiet and mostly vacant classroom. A student asks her to turn on the TV. Although we hear what the reporter says, the camera focuses on Banks. As the shock registers on her face, we're right there with her. And isn't that how it would happen? We're going about our business, oblivious to the outside, and then... we find out.

The viewer/protagonist connection continues the first time Banks enters the UFO and absorbs her reality. She struggles for breath in her oxygen mask and gazes up a dark passage that leads to a light source. You feel her uncertainty, her trepidation.

The tension carries over to the coal mine-like chamber in which the humans and aliens interact. A bird's echoing chirps – the bird confirms oxygen levels – create a jarring sensation as Banks and Donnelly first approach the bright transparent screen that separates them from the aliens.

Language Twisting and Time Bending
Many films offer sleek alien craft and creatures that resemble octopuses – this film refers to them as "heptapods" (and Abbott and Costello) – but rarely are these conventions used in such a thematically inventive way.

The film's first major theme is language and, more broadly, communication. While Banks and Donnelly race to translate the aliens' complex symbols, some other countries elect to communicate with the visitors via games. Banks points out the flaw in this strategy: games have winners and losers. This human winner/loser or good/bad mentality takes root in certain individuals and nations that have a trigger-happy attitude toward the aliens. It's sad to think that some people would actually think the Earth would stand a chance: if aliens figure out how to get here, then they're more advanced than us.

The circular shape of the aliens' symbols ties into the film's other major theme: time. We're accustomed to thinking of time as linear. *Arrival*, applying that circular concept to its structure, trounces on that tendency and challenges us to see the bigger picture.

Language and time also played a role in my coming to understand this film. Admittedly, my wife and I didn't quite grasp the full meaning of what happened right away, but we discussed it – you could say we *circled* around it – for 45 minutes. Gradually, the pieces came together. And the tool that we used to achieve our arrival? Language. *Douglas J. Ogurek*
★★★★★

Doctor Strange, by Jon Spaihts, Scott Derrickson and C. Robert Cargill (Marvel Studios)

Top-notch acting meets special effects in world-hopping tale of narcissist's downfall and rebirth.

Full disclosure: I am not a comic book nerd, and I knew nothing about Doctor Strange before seeing the latest Marvel blockbuster that bears his name. I am, however, quite familiar with the acting talents of Benedict Cumberbatch, Tilda Swinton, and Chiwetel Ejiofor. So it was with great enthusiasm that I anticipated this superhero origin film. The wait paid off.

Doctor Strange, directed by Scott Derrickson, takes to the next level the twisted cityscapes of *Inception* (2010) while detailing the collapse and reinvention of a gifted a-hole who loses sight of his own capacity for error. As the protagonist undertakes a journey both physical and spiritual, the themes that emerge include Western versus Eastern values and black-and-white thinking versus contextualism.

He Had It Coming

Doctor Stephen Strange (Cumberbatch) is a god of Western medicine, a highly demanded neurosurgeon with smooth hands and a photographic memory. He is precise, calm, brilliant, and in control. However, Strange is also a cold-hearted narcissist. He puts down those who question him and turns down patients if helping them won't bring him recognition. He treats on-again, off-again love interest and fellow surgeon Christine Palmer (Rachel McAdams) like a pair of latex gloves. He's also a slave to time because he wants to solidify his name in the annals of medical history.

Then Strange gets in a horrible car accident that ruins his steady hands. On the advice of a fellow who miraculously recovered from a spinal injury, Strange heads to Katmandu, Nepal. He wants to get his hands fixed and get back into the brain game ASAP. He ends up in Kamar-Taj, where Mordor (Ejiofor) introduces him to The Ancient One (Swinton) and her followers, a secretive philosophical warrior group that uses "the mystic arts" to protect the world.

Strange gets sucked into the group's effort to stop

The Ancient One's wayward protégé Kaecilius (Mads Mikkelsen) from destroying the Earth. Kaecilius has formed an alliance with Dark Dimension ruler Dormammu, who sees the Earth as a trophy in his quest to take over the multiverse. In exchange for eternal life, Kaecilius helps Dormammu.

True to Marvel form, there's some comic relief. For instance, Strange repeatedly and unsuccessfully attempts to get super-serious librarian Wong to laugh. "Wong?" he asks. "Just Wong? Like Adele?" Then there's the temperamental Cloak of Levitation that Strange encounters. It tugs Strange around like a child and flaps and twists as it cartoonishly dispatches an enemy.

She's Complicated

Surely the most enigmatic character in this film is The Ancient One. When Stephen "I do not believe in fairy tales" Strange first encounters her, he's skeptical of her Eastern approach. He's seen her spiritual body charts in "gift shops".

The Ancient One, slow to anger, finds his insults amusing and quickly shows him her capabilities. What makes The Ancient One so captivating is her contextual approach to problems. She's prone to ask herself what makes the most sense in a given situation to best serve the greater good. Thus, The Ancient One bends entire cities, but she also bends the rules. Strange eventually sums her up well: "She's complicated." Her way of thinking will play a key role in this story and in Strange's transformation.

In a brilliant reversal, the filmmakers give a nod to The Ancient One's philosophy by casting a female in a role traditionally depicted as male.

Change Is Good

During a physical therapy session, Strange contemptuously refers to his therapist as "Bachelor's

Degree". This is the kind of guy we want to watch! We can't necessarily relate to a neurosurgeon, but we can relate to selfish behaviour.

Doctor Strange is, at its core, a study in overcoming closedmindedness. "You cannot beat a river into submission," says The Ancient One. "You have to surrender to its current and use its power as your own."

Strange's fall is a big one, and Cumberbatch effectively welcomes the viewer to the protagonist's journey. The character's shaking hands and his unyielding determination help achieve viewer empathy; it's a pleasure to go on this journey with him. You want him to grow, and you want to grow with him. *Douglas J. Ogurek* ★★★★★

Television

Supernatural, Season 11, by Andrew Dabb, Jenny Klein, Robert Berens and chums (E4)

Supernatural season 11 may not be different from what we have seen before, but it's enjoyable as ever. Sam and Dean continue to investigate murders, in the "monster of the week episodes", and we see the return of strong female characters Sheriff Mills and Sheriff Donna, adding a female presence to the programme. There is also a new threat to the world and the Winchester brothers must find a way (with the help of some great returning characters – Castiel and Crowley) to defeat this new evil. The cast's chemistry as an ensemble is a real highlight. The script is witty and the back and forth banter between the Winchester brothers and especially Castiel is superb. Misha Collins's performance is just marvellous this season. A standout episode is "Just My Imagination", episode 8. Sam and Dean team up with Sam's

childhood imaginary friend; such a clever idea. In
episode 14, "The Vessel", Sam and Dean go back in
time and we learn more about the Men of Letters.
These individual episodes really add to the strength of
the ongoing story arcs and made this season well
worth watching. The fantastic season finale, "Alpha
and Omega", introduces a new female character who
brings the promise of international adventures. The
programme is still going strong and I'm enjoying it as
much as I did when it started over a decade ago. *Rose
M. Rye* ★★★★☆

Notes

Also Read

Notes by Stephen Theaker

Much as I'd like to review everything I read, there isn't time, especially when I plough through a pile of comics over a weekend! During 2016, especially, I read a huge number of graphic novels and trade paperbacks, thanks to Humble Bundles and sales on Comixology, and then thanks to a silly (but successful!) attempt to finish three hundred books in a year. Here then, as a special "treat", is a round-up of everything I read but didn't have time to review, plus ratings for books I reviewed for other publications. The credited writers and publishers here are mostly taken from Goodreads, and haven't been checked against the actual books, so apologies to anyone who is miscredited or missing.

Adventure Time, Vol. 5, by Ryan North et al. (Titan Comics). ★★★★☆

Adventure Time, Vol. 7, by Ryan North, Shelli Paroline, Braden Lamb, et al. (KaBOOM!). Stunningly good comics about Finn, Jake and all their little pals. These set a bar for tie-ins so high that it's hard to think of anything that matches it. ★★★★★

Adventure Time: Bitter Sweets, by Kate Leth, Zack Sterling, Meredith McClaren (KaBOOM!). ★★★★☆

Agra Aska, by D.F. Lewis (self-published). Signed copy from the author!

Alien vs. Predator: Thrill of the Hunt, by Mike Kennedy and Roger Robinson (Dark Horse). ★★☆☆☆

Aliens: Fast Track to Heaven, by Liam Sharp (Dark Horse). An original graphic novel. ★★★☆☆

All-New X-Men, Vol. 1: Yesterday's X-Men, by Brian Michael Bendis, Stuart Immonen, Wade Von Grawbadger, et al. (Marvel). The 3300th book I read (more or less). Because the present-day X-Men are in such a bad state, Beast brings the original X-Men forward in time to have a quick word – but they decide to stay. Not sure yet about Stuart Immonen's new art style – I loved his work on Superman. ★★★☆☆

All-New X-Men, Vol. 2: Here to Stay, by Brian Michael Bendis, David Marquez, Stuart Immonen, et al. (Marvel). ★★★☆☆

All-New X-Men, Vol. 3: Out of Their Depth, by Brian Michael Bendis, Stuart Immonen, Wade Von Grawbadger, et al. (Marvel). ★★★☆☆

All-New X-Men, Vol. 4: All-Different, by Brian Michael Bendis, Stuart Immonen, Wade Von Grawbadger, Brandon Peterson, Mahmud Asrar, Brent Anderson (Marvel). ★★★☆☆

All-New X-Men, Vol. 5: One Down, by Brian Michael Bendis, Stuart Immonen, Wade Von Grawbadger, et al. (Marvel). A disappointing series that started off well, bringing the original X-Men to the present, then quickly lost interest in that premise and got embroiled in a bunch of crossovers, the muddle made worse by the crossover issues being left out of the collections altogether. ★★★☆☆

All-New X-Men, Vol. 6: The Ultimate Adventure, by Brian Michael Bendis, Mahmud Asrar, Stuart Immonen, et al. (Marvel). ★★★☆☆

All-New X-Men, Vol. 7: The Utopians, by Brian Michael Bendis, Mahmud Asrar, Andrea Sorrentino, et al. (Marvel). Disappointing end to a series that began with some promise. ★★☆☆☆

The Amazing Spider-Man: The Complete Clone

Saga Epic, Vol. 1, by J.M. DeMatteis, Tom DeFalco, Howard Mackie, et al. (Marvel). A long book collecting the earliest episodes from the period when Spider-Man's clone (if that's what he is) turned up. I think they missed a trick here, because the clone has a bad attitude, but at this time so does Spider-Man, big-time – he's just calling himself the Spider, and not even living as Peter Parker any more. It would have been so much more fun if the clone had still had the jolly outlook of the young Peter Parker. And while I have some sympathy for the clone, having memories of Peter Parker's life but not feeling that he has a right to the love of Mary Jane and Aunt May, the extent to which this affects his everyday behaviour feels a bit overdone. ★★★☆☆

Amityville Horrible, by Kelley Armstrong (Subterranean Press). Novella about a real psychic pretending to be a fake psychic who goes on a reality ghosthunting show, expecting it to be fake but discovering a real ghost. Good though it had some *very* saucy bits. ★★★☆☆

The Areas of My Expertise, by John Hodgman (Riverhead Trade). Invented facts that add up to a fantastical alternate history of the USA, in which Hawaii is what remains of the mountain peaks of Mu, bourbon comes from the mines of Kentucky, and Jupiter is a moon of the largest planet Gigantor. Enjoyed it very much, but might have enjoyed it even more if I'd been more familiar with the American history it was riffing on. ★★★★☆

Artifacts, Vol. 1, by Ron Marz et al. (Image Comics). Poor crossover comic forcing the various Top Cow pin-up properties into one story. ★☆☆☆☆

Asterix and the Missing Scroll, by Jean-Yves Ferri,

Didier Conrad (Orion). A bit of a let-down after the previous book was so good. ★★☆☆☆

Avengers: Endless Wartime, by Warren Ellis and Mike McKone (Marvel). I had high hopes for this – within Marvel comics continuity, it adds Wolverine and Captain Marvel to the characters who appeared in the Avengers films – but it just wasn't very much fun. ★★☆☆☆

Babette's Feast, by Isak Dinesen (Karen Blixen) (Penguin). One of many excellent Penguin Mini Moderns I read in 2016. ★★★★☆

The Bad Beginning, by Lemony Snicket (Scholastic). I originally bought this because it is by the accordian player in the Magnetic Fields. ★★★★☆

Batman: Bruce Wayne, Murderer? by Greg Rucka, Kelley Puckett, Chuck Dixon, et al. (DC Comics). Incomplete but enjoyable. Bruce Wayne is yet again framed for murder, and allows himself to be put in prison. His super-friends want to break him out but he declines. ★★★★☆

BFS Journal #15, ed. by Allen Stroud (British Fantasy Society). Although I didn't have any involvement with this, except for writing a news item about the British Fantasy Awards, I was on the BFS committee when this came out, so I won't give it a star rating – I'd be biased. It's an interesting, more academic direction for the journal, and a good solid read. It's not as polished as it could have been, with pretty bad errors throughout, but the editor explains it was produced in a rush, and seen in that light it's a good start. The articles are decent, though one about a Clive Barker video game gave the distinct impression that the writer had only played the first ten minutes and based the entire essay on those. A report from FantasyCon was my favourite piece, following the traditional trend for FantasyCon reportees to miss practically everything but have a good time anyway.

Binti, by Nnedi Okorafor (Tor.com). An excellent novella about a young woman who leaves home to study on another world, only for the spaceship she is on to be viciously attacked by aliens. ★★★★☆

Bitch Planet, Vol. 1: Extraordinary Machine, by Kelly Sue DeConnick, Valentine De Landro and Robert Wilson IV (Image Comics). Terrific 2000AD-style story of women sent to a prison on another planet. ★★★★☆

Blackest Night, by Geoff Johns, Ivan Reis, Oclair Albert, et al. (DC Comics). The dead rise, in a Green Lantern epic! ★★★☆☆

Bloodshot Reborn: Deluxe Edition, Book 1, by Jeff Lemire, Mico Suayan, Butch Guice, et al. (Valiant). Review to follow in TQF59.

Brightest Day, Vol. 2, by Geoff Johns, Peter J. Tomasi, Ivan Reis, et al. (DC Comics). Big crossover story for lots of second-string characters. ★★★☆☆

Brightest Day, Vol. 3, by Geoff Johns, Peter J. Tomasi, Ivan Reis, et al. (DC Comics). It's okay. ★★★☆☆

Buffy the Vampire Slayer Season 10, Vol. 1: New Rules, by Christos Gage, Nicholas Brendon, Rebekah Isaacs, et al. (Dark Horse). ★★★☆☆

The Caped Crusade: Batman and the Rise of Nerd Culture, by Glen Weldon (Simon & Schuster). An excellent overview of the Dark Knight's career both on and off the page, by an NPR journalist, a regular contributor to the excellent Pop Culture Happy Hour podcast. Reviewed for *Interzone* #264. ★★★★☆

Clive Barker: Mythmaker for the Millennium, by

Suzanne J. Barbieri (British Fantasy Society). Highly pretentious but glad I read it. ★★☆☆☆

Cravan: Mystery Man of the Twentieth Century, by Mike Richardson, Rick Geary (Dark Horse). Biographical but not necessarily reliable comic about a highly unusual life. Cravan was a nephew of Oscar Wilde who became a controversial figure on the Parisian art scene. The book suggests he faked his death and became B. Traven, the secretive author of *The Treasure of the Sierra Madre*. ★★★★☆

Crisis on Multiple Earths, Vol. 1, by Gardner F. Fox, Mike Sekowsky, Bernard Sachs, et al. (DC Comics). Crossovers between Earth-1 (the Justice League of America) and Earth-2 (the Justice Society of America). ★★★☆☆

Crisis on Multiple Earths, Vol. 3, by Mike Friedrich, Len Wein, Dick Dillin, et al. (DC Comics). ★★★★☆

Cut, by Mike Richardson, Al Milgrom, Todd Herman (Dark Horse). ★★★☆☆

The Cute Manifesto, by James Kochalka (Alternative Comics). Non-fiction work, including his famous declaration that craft is the enemy – i.e. the best way to learn to make stuff is to get on with making it, and do it over and over till you get good at it. Doesn't take long to read, but it'll stick with you. ★★★★☆

Dark Matter, Vol. 1: Rebirth, by Joseph Mallozzi, Garry Brown, Ryan Brown, et al. (Dark Horse). A bunch of people wake up on a spaceship with no memory of how they got there. Now a television show. ★★★☆☆

The Darkness: Accursed, Vol. 7, by Phil Hester, Romano Molenaar, Leandro Oliveira, et al. (Image Comics). Top Cow books aren't really for me. ★★★☆☆

Darth Vader and Son, by Jeffrey Brown (Chronicle Books). Very funny Star Wars cartoons from the author of *Incredible Change-Bots*, reviewed back in TQF39. The massive success of this book shows how totally wrong I was when I said that children "probably wouldn't understand the appeal of the art style"! ★★★★☆

Deep Gravity, by Gabriel Hardman, Corinna Sara Bechko, Mike Richardson (Dark Horse). ★★★☆☆

Doctor Who: The Beast of Babylon, by Charlie Higson (Puffin). The Doctor seems a bit blasé about killing in this one, and even a bit off-colour when he talks about humans having humanity. ★★☆☆☆

Doctor Who: Big Hand for The Doctor, by Eoin Colfer (Puffin). Another one where the Doctor seems rather out of character: this time it's an all-action first Doctor! ★★☆☆☆

Doctor Who: The Emperor Dalek's New Clothes, by Justin Richards (Puffin). Short fairy-tale story about rebels attacking dalek invaders. ★★★☆☆

Doctor Who: Little Rose Riding Hood, by Justin Richards (Puffin). Could have done with a glass of water before reading this to the children, but I suppose that helped with my raspy Zygon voice. ★★★☆☆

Doctor Who: The Mystery of the Haunted Cottage, by Derek Landy (Puffin). The Doctor and Martha in an Enid Blyton-inspired world of the imagination. But whose imagination? ★★★☆☆

Doctor Who: The Nameless City, by Michael Scott (Puffin). ★★★☆☆

Doctor Who: Nothing O'Clock, by Neil Gaiman (Puffin). Probably the best of these little Doctor Who books. Aliens take over the Earth, perfectly legally. Would make a great television episode. ★★★★☆

Doctor Who: Snow White and the Seven Keys to Doomsday, by Justin Richards (Puffin). ★★★☆☆

Doctor Who: The Spear of Destiny, by Marcus Sedgwick (Puffin). ★★★☆☆

Doctor Who: Spore, by Alex Scarrow (Puffin). ★★★☆☆

Doctor Who: Tip of the Tongue, by Patrick Ness (Puffin). ★★★★☆

The Dragon Griaule, by Lucius Shepard (Gollancz). One of the best books I read in 2016. Collects a series of excellent novellas set in the area around a gigantic sleeping dragon that subtly affects the thoughts of all who come too close. ★★★★★

Eerie Presents El Cid, by Budd Lewis, Philip Simon, Gonzalo Mayo, et al. (Dark Horse). A fantastical take on the legendary Spanish hero. ★★☆☆☆

Ex Machina Book One, by Brian K. Vaughan, Tony Harris (Vertigo). ★★★★☆

Ex Machina Book Two, by Brian K. Vaughan, Tony Harris, Chris Sprouse (Vertigo). ★★★★☆

Ex Machina Book Three, by Brian K. Vaughan, Tony Harris, John Paul Leon (Vertigo). ★★★★☆

Ex Machina Book Four, by Brian K. Vaughan, Tony Harris (Vertigo). ★★★☆☆

Ex Machina Book Five, by Brian K. Vaughan, Tony Harris, John Paul Leon (Vertigo). It was really nice to read all of this in order at last. ★★★☆☆

Fantastic Beasts and Where to Find Them, by Newt Scamander, J.K. Rowling (Bloomsbury). ★★★☆☆

Fantastic Beasts and Where to Find Them: The Original Screenplay, by J.K. Rowling (Pottermore). Astonishingly similar to the final film, right down to every line, every cut, and every scene transition. Either the director was amazingly faithful, or the script was edited to match the finished movie. ★★★★☆

Fatale, Vol. 2: The Devil's Business, by Ed Brubaker, Sean Phillips and Dave Stewart (Image Comics). Cthulhu noir. ★★★☆☆

Father's Day, by Mike Richardson, Gabriel Guzman (Dark Horse). ★★★☆☆

Fine, Fine, Fine, Fine, Fine, by Diane Williams (McSweeney's). Bright yellow collection of super-short stories. ★★★★☆

Forge #9, by Mark Alessi, CrossGen Comics Staff (CrossGen). I used to really like CrossGen. I liked the way you could subscribe and read their comics online, and the way they put out these cheap but glossy paperback anthologies collecting their comics. ★★★☆☆

The Four Thousand, the Eight Hundred, by Greg Egan (Subterranean Press). Review to follow in TQF59.

The Goon, Vol. 6: Chinatown & the Mystery of Mr. Wicker, by Eric Powell (Dark Horse). ★★★☆☆

Green Lantern: Rise of the Third Army, by Geoff Johns, Peter Milligan, Doug Mahnke, et al. (DC Comics). The Guardians are little blue aliens who have been trying to bring peace and stability to the universe, for which they receive very little thanks, for millennia. The Manhunters were their first army, but they proved rather inflexible. The Green Lanterns were their second army, but they were too willful. Thus came the Third Army, grown from the Guardians' own flesh and powered by the energies of the mysterious

First Lantern. Mindless pale drones with incredible strength, they travel freely through space to assimilate all life. Most convert easily, others die, and the Lanterns can only be turned once their will has been conquered and their ring-bearing arms ripped off. ★★★☆☆

Grendel Omnibus, Vol. 1: Hunter Rose, by Matt Wagner, Guy Davis, Mike Allred, et al. (Dark Horse). ★★★★☆

Groo: Friends and Foes, Vol. 2, by Sergio Aragonés, Mark Evanier (Dark Horse). ★★★★☆

Groo: Friends and Foes, Vol. 3, by Sergio Aragonés, Mark Evanier, Tom Luth, Michael Atiyeh (Dark Horse). Some of Sergio's very best work. ★★★★★

Harry Potter and the Cursed Child – Parts One and Two, by John Tiffany, Jack Thorne, J.K. Rowling (Little, Brown UK). ★★★★☆

Harry Potter and the Deathly Hallows, by J.K. Rowling (Bloomsbury). Took me a while, but I finally finished it. The littlest Theaker and I sat and read the last chapter in tandem, which is something I'll never forget. It's her enthusiasm that got me to read all these Potter books this year: she was desperate for someone she could talk to them about without worrying about spoilers. The battle at the end was terrific. ★★★★★

Hell Screen, by Ryanosuke Akutagawa (Penguin). ★★★★☆

Hogwarts: An Incomplete and Unreliable Guide, by J.K. Rowling (Pottermore). ★★★☆☆

Hollow Fields, Vol. 1, by Madeleine Rosca (Seven Seas). Cute manga about a regular girl who accidentally starts attending a school for the children of evil geniuses. No idea how I came to own this! ★★★☆☆

Hunters & Collectors, by M. Suddain (Jonathan Cape). Reviewed in *Interzone* #265. The horrific adventures of the world's most famous food critic. A lot like a prose version of *Transmetropolitan*. ★★★☆☆

The Hypernaturals, Vol. 1, by Dan Abnett, Andy Lanning, Brad Walker et al. (BOOM). ★★★☆☆

I Am Providence, by Nick Mamatas (Night Shade Books). About a writer murdered at a Lovecraft convention. Review to follow in TQF59.

I Murdered My Library, by Linda Grant (Amazon). A sad true-life tale of what it's like to discard a lot of your books. It's a shame they aren't like CDs, games and DVDs, where you can throw out the packaging and keep the content. ★★★★☆

I Travel by Night, by Robert McCammon (Subterranean Press). Average novella about a vampire gunslinger. ★★☆☆☆

In the Penal Colony, by Franz Kafka (Penguin). ★★★★☆

Invisible Republic, Vol. 1, by Gabriel Hardman, Corinna Sara Bechko, Jordan Boyd, et al. (Image Comics). A journalist on the skids finds the journal of a dictator's old friend, a woman who was scrubbed from the official histories. ★★★☆☆

Itty Bitty Mask, by Art Baltazar, Franco (Dark Horse). Very much for children. ★★★☆☆

Judge Dredd: The Complete Case Files 02, by John Wagner, Pat Mills, Chris Lowder, et al. (Rebellion). ★★★☆☆

Jupiter's Legacy, Vol. 1, by Mark Millar and Frank

Quitely (Image Comics). A bunch of young superhero jerks decide to kill off the Superman of their world so that they can do what they want. Pretty good.
★★★★☆

Kaijumax, Season 1, by Zander Cannon (Oni Press). Giant monsters in prison – *Destroy All Monsters* crossed with HBO's *Oz*. The artwork is cute, but the story is grim, and the combination can be very jarring.
★★★☆☆

King Tiger, by Randy Stradley, Doug Wheatley (Dark Horse). Decent enough adventure comic. ★★★☆☆

The Lantern Bearers, by Rosemary Sutcliff (Oxford University Press). Third in the Eagle of the Ninth series. In this one the last Roman soldier left in Britain gets captured by Jutes and made a thrall. This is basically post-apocalyptic fiction already – the apocalypse having just befallen the Roman Empire – but if Sutcliff wrote any outright fantasy or science fiction I'd love to read it. ★★★★★

Letters to Arkham: The Letters of Ramsey Campbell and August Derleth, 1961–1971, by Ramsey Campbell, August Derleth, ed. S.T. Joshi (PS Publishing). Review to follow in TQF59.

Locke & Key, Vol. 6: Alpha & Omega, by Joe Hill, Gabriel Rodriguez (IDW). ★★★★☆

The Marquis: Inferno, by Guy Davis (Dark Horse). A bit hard to follow at first, but worth the effort. A demon-hunter does his work in a city under the oppression of religious terror. ★★★★☆

Mass Effect: Redemption, by Mac Walters, Omar Francia, Michael Atiyeh, et al. (Dark Horse).
★★★☆☆

Metronome, by Oliver Langmead (Unsung Stories). Review to follow in TQF59.

More Information Than You Require, by John Hodgman (Dutton Adult). More fantastical non-facts. ★★★★☆

Mouse Guard, Vol. 2: Winter 1152, by David Petersen (Archaia). ★★★★☆

Mouse Guard, Vol. 3: The Black Axe, by David Petersen (Archaia). Well-crafted comic about a brave little mouse's quest to recover a legendary black axe from an island ruled by a ferret king. Might never have got around to reading this if I weren't hoovering up all my short books, but I'm glad I did. ★★★★☆

Ms. Marvel, Vol. 2: Generation Why, by G. Willow Wilson, Adrian Alphona and Jacob Wyatt (Marvel). More adventures for the admirable Kamala Khan. ★★★☆☆

Ms. Marvel, Vol. 3: Crushed, by G. Willow Wilson, Takeshi Miyazawa, Elmo Bondoc (Marvel). ★★★☆☆

Ms. Marvel, Vol. 4: Last Days, by G. Willow Wilson, Adrian Alphona (Marvel). What Ms. Marvel got up to in Jersey City while a big Marvel crossover event was going on. ★★★☆☆

Ms. Marvel, Vol. 5: Super Famous, by G. Willow Wilson, Takeshi Miyazawa, Adrian Alphona, et al. (Marvel). Kamala Khan is a great character, but the more you read of these stories, the more they feel like standard teen-orientated Marvel comics, the kind of thing *Spider-Girl* did a little bit better. ★★★☆☆

No Mercy, Vol. 1, by Alex de Campi, Carla Speed McNeil, Jenn Manley Lee (Image Comics). A bunch of teenagers on a trip to do charity work get stranded on a mountain. Probably wouldn't have bought this if I hadn't mistakenly thought it was a science fiction comic, but I still liked it. ★★★☆☆

The Pauper Prince and the Eucalyptus Jinn, by Usman T. Malik (Tor Books). ★★★★☆

Phonogram, Vol. 1: Rue Britannia, by Kieron Gillen, Jamie McKelvie (Image Comics). About magicians whose power is based in music. The main character draws on the power of Britpop, and his personality starts to change as someone starts messing with it. ★★★☆☆

Phonogram, Vol. 2: The Singles Club, by Kieron Gillen, Jamie McKelvie (Image Comics). Love music, love comics, but didn't love this combination of the two as much as I expected. Felt a bit like seeing a photo of myself at an indie disco and realising what a wally I was (and indeed still am). ★★★☆☆

Pirate Utopia, by Bruce Sterling (Tachyon Publications). Review to follow in TQF59.

Planet of the Apes, Vol. 2: The Devil's Pawn, by Daryl Gregory, Carlos Magno (BOOM! Studios). ★★★☆☆

Planet of the Apes, Vol. 3: Children of Fire, by Daryl Gregory, Carlos Magno (BOOM! Studios). ★★★☆☆

Planet of the Apes, Vol. 4: The Half Man, by Daryl Gregory, Carlos Magno, Jeff Parker, et al. (BOOM! Studios). ★★★☆☆

Plants vs. Zombies, Vol. 2: Timepocalypse, by Paul Tobin, Ron Chan (Dark Horse). A fan of the game would probably enjoy it. ★★★☆☆

Platinum Grit, Vol. 1, by Trudy Cooper, Danny Murphy (Image Comics). Goofball comedy about a guy who might inherit a castle if he survives a duel to the death with an immortal. ★★☆☆☆

Preacher, Book One, by Garth Ennis, Steve Dillon (Vertigo). I'd forgotten how much I enjoyed this the first time around. Still stands up, on the whole. ★★★★☆

Preacher, Book Two, by Garth Ennis, Steve Dillon (Vertigo). ★★★★☆

Predator: Prey to the Heavens, by John Arcudi, Javier Saltares and Wes Dzioba (Dark Horse). ★★☆☆☆

Project Black Sky: Secret Files, by Fred Van Lente and Michael Broussard (Dark Horse). ★★★☆☆

The Projected Girl, by Lavie Tidhar (Lurid Press). A really good novella. ★★★★☆

The Ragthorn, by Robert Holdstock and Garry Kilworth (infinity plus). Third in my quest to read a book by each of the four chaps who have British Fantasy Awards named after them, as a little farewell to that part of my life. This was the best of them so far. You have to admire authors who write a story about secret, excised portions of Chaucer and Shakespeare's work, and then have the confidence to write the missing parts themselves. ★★★★☆

The Rise of Io, by Wesley Chu (Angry Robot). Reviewed for *Interzone* #266. Cyberpunk action with an appealing lead character. ★★★☆☆

Rising Stars: Compendium – Part 1, by J. Michael Straczynski, Various (Image Comics). A huge collection of the *Babylon 5* writer's comic about 113 people with superpowers, all from the same small town. The story is okay, but the artwork often makes it hard to read. ★★★☆☆

Rising Stars: Compendium – Part 2, by Fiona Avery, Dan Jurgens, Jason Gorder, et al. (Image Comics). ★★★☆☆

Saga, Vol. 3, by Brian K. Vaughan and Fiona Staples (Image Comics). ★★★★☆

Saga, Vol. 4, by Brian K. Vaughan and Fiona Staples (Image Comics). ★★★★☆

Saga, Vol. 5, by Brian K. Vaughan and Fiona Staples (Image Comics). ★★★★☆

Saga, Vol. 6, by Brian K. Vaughan and Fiona Staples (Image Comics). ★★★☆☆

Savage Dragon Archives, Vol. 2, by Erik Larsen (Image Comics). ★★★☆☆

Savage Dragon Archives, Vol. 3, by Erik Larsen (Image Comics). ★★★★☆

Savage Dragon Archives, Vol. 4, by Erik Larsen (Image Comics). ★★★★☆

Savage Dragon Archives, Vol. 5, by Erik Larsen (Image Comics). ★★★☆☆

Savage Dragon Archives, Vol. 6, by Erik Larsen (Image Comics). Another big black-and-white collection of twenty-five issues. I read five of these in a row, and it was very good fun. They're very inventive and energetic. ★★★☆☆

The Savage Sword of Conan, Vol. 14, by Chuck Dixon, Chris Warner, Gary Kwapisz, Ernie Chan (Dark Horse). ★★★★☆

The Secret, by Mike Richardson, Jason Alexander (Dark Horse). A bunch of teenagers phone up random numbers and say, "I know your secret." With terrible consequences. ★★★☆☆

Short Stories from Hogwarts of Heroism,

Hardship and Dangerous Hobbies, by J.K. Rowling (Pottermore). ★★★☆☆

Short Stories from Hogwarts of Power, Politics and Pesky Poltergeists, by J.K. Rowling (Pottermore). ★★★☆☆

Sin City, Vol. 7: Hell and Back, by Frank Miller (Dark Horse). ★★★★☆

Six-Gun Gorilla, by Simon Spurrier, Jeff Stokely, Andre May, Steve Wands (BOOM! Studios). ★★★★☆

Skyman, Vol. 1: The Right Stuff, by Joshua Hale Fialkov, Manuel Garcia, Javier Bergantino Menor, et al. (Dark Horse). ★★★☆☆

The Snobs, by Muriel Spark (Penguin). Brilliant short stories, some with a bit of fantasy. ★★★★★

Spider-Verse, by Dan Slott, Christos Gage, David Hine, et al. (Marvel). A fun crossover with Spider-men and women from across the multiverse, coming together in response to being hunted. ★★★☆☆

Spyboy, Vol. 1: The Deadly Gourmet Affair, by Peter David, Pop Mhan and Norman Lee (Dark Horse). I'm usually a fan of Peter David's humour, but this series didn't work for me. Already feels very dated. ★★☆☆☆

Spyboy, Vol. 2: Trial and Terror, by Peter David et al. (Dark Horse). ★★☆☆☆

Spyboy, Vol. 3: Bet Your Life, by Peter David, Carlos Meglia, Pop Mhan (Dark Horse). ★★☆☆☆

Star Trek Classics Vol. 1: The Gorn Crisis, by Kevin J. Anderson, Rebecca Moesta and Igor Kordey (IDW). ★★★☆☆

Star Trek Classics: The Next Generation: Enemy Unseen, by Keith R.A. DeCandido, Peter Pachoumis, Christopher Golden, et al. (IDW). You can tell how much of an impact this made from the fact that I read it all the way through without realising I'd read it all before. ★★★☆☆

Star Trek, Vol. 2, by Mike Johnson, Joe Corroney, Joe Phillips (IDW). ★★★☆☆

Star Trek, Vol. 3, by Mike Johnson, Stephen Molnar, Claudia Balboni, et al. (IDW). ★★★☆☆

Star Trek, Vol. 4, by Mike Johnson, Stephen Molnar (IDW). ★★★☆☆

Star Trek, Vol. 5, by Mike Johnson, Ryan Parrott, Claudia Balboni (IDW). ★★★☆☆

Star Trek, Vol. 6: After Darkness, by Mike Johnson, Ryan Parrott (IDW). I liked that the comics kept Carol Marcus on the crew after the events of *Star Trek Into Darkness*. ★★★☆☆

Star Trek, Vol. 7, by Mike Johnson, Erfan Fajar (IDW). ★★★☆☆

Star Trek, Vol. 8, by Mike Johnson, Yasmin Liang, Erfan Fajar (IDW). ★★★☆☆

Star Trek, Vol. 9: The Q Gambit, by Mike Johnson, Tony Shasteen (IDW). ★★★☆☆

Star Trek, Vol. 10, by Mike Johnson, Cat Staggs, Tony Shasteen, Wes Hartman, Davide Mastrolonardo, Neil Uyetake (IDW). ★★★☆☆

Star Trek, Vol. 11, by Mike Johnson, Scott Tipton, David Tipton, Rachael Stott, Tony Shasteen, Sharp Bros (IDW). It may seem surprising that I bought and read so much of a series I was fairly lukewarm about, but I got them all in a Humble Bundle and read a lot of them in a single afternoon. ★★★☆☆

Star Trek/Green Lantern: The Spectrum War, by

Mike Johnson, Stephen Molnar, Tamra Bonvillain, et al. (IDW). A poor crossover. ★★☆☆☆

Star Trek: Assignment Earth, by John Byrne, Tom Smith (IDW). Based on a proposed *Star Trek* spin-off that never got off the ground. ★★★☆☆

Star Trek: Harlan Ellison's The City on the Edge of Forever: The Original Teleplay, by Harlan Ellison, Scott Tipton, David Tipton, et al. (IDW). Interesting to read, with some very nice art, but I still think I preferred the original episode. ★★★☆☆

Star Trek: Khan, by Mike Johnson and Claudia Balboni (IDW). Explains why Khan didn't look Indian (or indeed Mexican) in *Star Trek Into Darkness*. ★★★☆☆

Star Trek: New Visions, Vol. 2, by John Byrne (IDW). Interesting idea: new stories of the original crew, created using photos of them. ★★★☆☆

Star Trek: New Visions, Vol. 3, by John Byrne (IDW). Best of the three so far, though it's the technical ingenuity I appreciate as much as the stories. ★★★☆☆

Star Trek: Spock Reflections, by Scott Tipton, David Tipton (IDW). ★★★☆☆

Star Wars Omnibus: A Long Time Ago...., Vol. 2, by Archie Goodwin, Chris Claremont, Michael Golden, Terry Austin, Al Williamson, Walter Simonson (Dark Horse). ★★★☆☆

Stet: An Editor's Life, by Diana Athill (Grove Press). A present from my co-editor John and his wonderful family! A fascinating book about the life of an editor who worked with big names like V.S. Naipaul and Jean Rhys, with scandalous stories about them all. ★★★★☆

Strangers in Paradise, Vol. 1, by Terry Moore (Abstract Studio). Not fantasy, it turns out. ★★★☆☆

Suicide Risk, Vol. 1, by Mike Carey, Elena Casagrande (BOOM! Studios). ★★★☆☆

Suicide Risk, Vol. 2, by Mike Carey, Elena Casagrande, Joelle Jones (BOOM! Studios). ★★★☆☆

The Tales of Beedle the Bard, by J.K. Rowling (Bloomsbury). Short fairy stories from the wizarding world. ★★★★☆

Tales of the Batman: Len Wein, by Len Wein, Jim Aparo (DC Comics). Enjoyable Batman stories from when he was starting to look like a modern Batman but still talked like a sixties Batman. ★★★☆☆

A Taste of Honey, by Kai Ashante Wilson (Tor.com). Review to follow in TQF59.

Think Tank, Vol. 1, by Matt Hawkins, Rahsan Ekedal (Image Comics). An engineering genius escapes from a government think tank. ★★★☆☆

The Third Policeman, by Flann O'Brien (Harper Perennial). Another present from my co-editor. Reminded me a lot of *Lost* – e.g. weird guys in an underground office taking measurements of reality, and a threatening ghostly figure in an abandoned house – and apparently it was an influence on the show. ★★★★☆

Toast on Toast: Cautionary Tales and Candid Advice, by Steven Toast (Canongate). Britain's finest actor recounts his many triumphs. ★★★★☆

Transmetropolitan, Vol 1: Back on the Street, by Warren Ellis, Darick Robertson (Vertigo). ★★★★☆

Transmetropolitan, Vol. 2: Lust for Life, by Warren

Ellis, Darick Robertson and Rodney Ramos (Vertigo). ★★★★☆

Transmetropolitan, Vol. 3: Year of the Bastard, by Warren Ellis and Darick Robertson (Vertigo). ★★★★☆

Transmetropolitan, Vol. 4: The New Scum, by Warren Ellis and Darick Robertson (Vertigo). ★★★★☆

Transmetropolitan, Vol. 5: Lonely City, by Warren Ellis and Darick Robertson (Vertigo). ★★★★☆

Transmetropolitan, Vol. 6: Gouge Away, by Warren Ellis and Darick Robertson (Vertigo). ★★★★☆

Transmetropolitan, Vol. 7: Spider's Thrash, by Warren Ellis and Darick Robertson (DC Comics). ★★★★☆

Transmetropolitan, Vol. 8: Dirge, by Warren Ellis and Darick Robertson (DC Comics). ★★★★☆

Transmetropolitan, Vol. 9: The Cure, by Warren Ellis and Darick Robertson (Vertigo). ★★★★☆

Transmetropolitan, Vol. 10: One More Time, by Warren Ellis, Darick Robertson and Rodney Ramos (Vertigo). A great ending. ★★★★★

Two Past Midnight, by Duane Swiercynski, Eduardo Francisco, Stefani Rennee, et al. (Dark Horse). A decent stab at a crossover between three fairly incompatible characters: Ghost, X and Captain Midnight. ★★★☆☆

The Umbrella Academy, Vol. 2: Dallas, by Gerard Way, Gabriel Bã, Dave Stewart, et al. (Dark Horse). Written by the singer from My Chemical Romance. Much better than the comic by the chap from Fall Out Boy. ★★★☆☆

The Unbeatable Squirrel Girl, Vol. 1: Squirrel Power, by Ryan North, Erica Henderson (Marvel). A very likeable character. ★★★☆☆

Usagi Yojimbo: Yokai, by Stan Sakai (Dark Horse). A brilliant fully-painted story from Stan Sakai. ★★★★☆

Vader's Little Princess, by Jeffrey Brown (Chronicle Books). I enjoyed Jeffrey Brown's *Incredible Change-Bots* a few years back, but I could never have foreseen what a publishing sensation he would become with these books. ★★★★☆

Village Year: A Sac Prairie Journal, by August Derleth (August Derleth Society). My 200th book of the year, and the second book of my BFA reading challenge (to read a book by each of the four men BFAs are named after: Wagner, Derleth, Holdstock and Bounds). It's a beautifully written and highly relaxing account of life (and death) in a quirky little town (add a pair of garrulous young women and you'd have yourself a *Gilmore Girls*), as well as in the countryside around it (although reading *Letters to Arkham* made me realise the extent to which this was a redacted version of Derleth's somewhat scandalous life). Unfortunately it's one of those books that's been scanned in, not checked, and published anyway, so there are constant mistakes that often obscure the meaning. Never mind spinning in his grave, Derleth will be shambling up to the publisher's doorstep in the middle of the night... ★★★☆☆

The Walking Dead, Vol. 24: Life and Death, by Robert Kirkman, Charlie Adlard, Stefano Gaudiano, et al. (Image Comics). ★★★★☆

The Walking Dead, Vol. 25: No Turning Back, by Robert Kirkman, Charlie Adlard, Stefano Gaudiano (Image Comics). ★★★★☆

The Walking Dead, Vol. 26: Call to Arms, by Robert Kirkman, Charlie Adlard, Stefano Gaudiano (Image Comics). These take very little time to read, but always have a huge impact. ★★★★☆

Wicked Weeds: A Zombie Novel, by Pedro Cabiya, translated by Jessica Ernst Powell (Mandel Vilar Press). Reviewed in *Interzone* #267. Readers are encouraged to choose their own adventure, either by reading the book from front to back as usual, or by following the order given on the contents page. I went for the latter. ★★★☆☆

Witch Child, by Celia Rees (Bloomsbury). After her mentor is executed for witchcraft, a girl with supernatural powers travels to Salem... Bad choice! ★★★☆☆

A Wizard's Henchman, by Matthew Hughes (PS Publishing). Review to follow in TQF59.

Working Wonders, by Jenny Colgan (Harper). A town planning office putting together a bid for European City of Culture gets tangled up with Arthurian legend, as a descendant of King Arthur meets a mystic Lynne, is seduced by a duplicitous Fay and loses a beautiful Gwyneth. The fantasy elements seem to have made this very unpopular on Goodreads, but I liked it. ★★★☆☆

World of Water, by James Lovegrove (Solaris). Reviewed for *Interzone* #265. A smart science fiction blockbuster. Follow-up to *World of Fire*. Enjoyed them so much I bought them both for my dad as Father's Day presents. ★★★★☆

Y: The Last Man, Vol. 3: One Small Step, by Brian K. Vaughan, Pia Guerra, José Marzán Jr., et al. (Vertigo). ★★★★☆

Y: The Last Man, Vol. 5: Ring of Truth, by Brian K.

Vaughan, Pia Guerra and José Marzãn Jr. (Vertigo).
★★★★☆

Y: The Last Man, Vol. 6: Girl on Girl, by Brian K.
Vaughan and Pia Guerra (Vertigo). ★★★★☆

Y: The Last Man, Vol. 7: Paper Dolls, by Brian K.
Vaughan (Vertigo). ★★★★☆

Y: The Last Man, Vol. 8: Kimono Dragons, by Brian
K. Vaughan, Pia Guerra and José Marzãn Jr. (Vertigo).
★★★★☆

Y: The Last Man, Vol. 9: Motherland, by Brian K.
Vaughan, Pia Guerra (Vertigo). ★★★★☆

Y: The Last Man, Vol. 10: Whys and Wherefores, by
Brian K. Vaughan, Pia Guerra (Vertigo). An emotional
ending. ★★★★★

Young Miles, by Lois McMaster Bujold (Baen Books).
The story of Miles Vorkosigan, who joins the space
navy and gets himself into some very sticky situations,
but none so sticky that he can't talk his way out of
them. Very enjoyable. The way things work out in these
stories can be a bit pat, but sometimes that's just what
you're after. ★★★☆☆

Also Received, But Not Yet Reviewed
Notes by Stephen Theaker

- Bennett, J.A., *Music and the Tree Who Loved Her*
  (self-published): "Green was a seedling as proud as
  any conqueror..."
- Holloway, Verity, *Pseudotooth* (Unsung Stories):
  Aisling "is drawn to an unfamiliar town where the
  rule of Our Friend is absolute and those deemed
  unfit and undesirable disappear into The Quiet..."
- Langmead, Oliver, *Metronome* (Unsung Stories): "a
  world of impossible vistas, where reason is

banished and only the imagination holds sway: the connected worlds that all sleeping minds inhabit, and the doors that lead between".

- Mason, Zachary, *Void Star* (Jonathan Cape): "Those lucky enough to be rich in San Francisco are protected by weapons drones which patrol the skies to keep out the multitudinous poor."
- Palmer, Stephen, *The Girl with One Friend* (infinity plus)
- Palmer, Stephen, *The Girl with No Soul* (infinity plus)
- Palmer, Stephen, *The Girl with Two Souls* (infinity plus)
- Reed, Kit, *Little Sisters of the Apocalypse* (infinity plus)
- Stanger, Vaughan (ed.), *One Step Beyond* (self-published): published in support of English PEN
- Sterling, Bruce, *Pirate Utopia* (Tachyon Publications): "Perched near the pinnacle of Italy's boot, Carnaro is gripped in fanatical Futurism. Pirates, propagandists, Utopians, and libertines have banded together to create a brave new world." Review next issue!
- Tambour, Anna, *Monterra's Deliciosa & Other Tales &* (infinity plus)
- Tambour, Anna, *Spotted Lily* (infinity plus)
- Thompson, Arianne "Tex", *Dreams of the Eaten* (Solaris): saw this on NetGalley and couldn't resist requesting a book with such a great title!
- Tuttle, Lisa, *Lizard Lust* (infinity plus)
- Tuttle, Lisa, *The Bone Flute* (infinity plus)
- Tuttle, Lisa, *Closet Dreams* (infinity plus)
- Wyle, Karen A., *Who* (Oblique Angles Press): "After the young and vital Thea dies and is stored, her devoted husband Max starts to wonder about changes in her preoccupations and politics."

About TQF

Copyright

ISBN (print): 978-1-910387-21-4
ISBN (epub): 978-1-910387-22-1

ISSN (print): 1747-6083
ISSN (online): 1747-6075

Website: www.theakersquarterly.blogspot.com

Email: theakersquarterlyfiction@gmail.com

Lulu Store: www.lulu.com/silveragebooks

Feedbooks: www.feedbooks.com/userbooks/tag/tqf

Submissions: Submissions are very welcome! See website for guidelines and terms and reading periods.

Advertising: We welcome ad swaps with small press publishers and other creative types, and we'll run ads for relevant new projects from former contributors.

Sending material for review: We are happy to look at anything that's fantasy-related. We prefer to receive books for review in epub or mobi format, and comics in pdf. Feel free to send ebooks without querying first, but it's fair to warn you that we've only reviewed about 15% of items received since 2011, and even then that's mainly been stuff we've actively requested from places like NetGalley.

Mission statement: The primary goal of *Theaker's Quarterly Fiction* is to keep going. If you're wondering why we do something a particular way, our primary goal is probably why.

Published in Theaker's Paperback Library during February 2017.

Other Publications

Theaker's Quarterly Fiction
Stephen Theaker (ed.) *(#1–54, 56–57)*
John Greenwood (ed.) *(#9–54, 56–57)*
Howard Watts (ed.) *(#55)*

The Conan Doyle Weirdbook (ed.)
The Adventures of Roderick Langham (forthcoming)
Rafe McGregor

Space University Trent: Hyperparasite
Walt Brunston

There Are Now a Billion Flowers
The Hatchling (forthcoming)
John Greenwood

The Mercury Annual
Pilgrims at the White Horizon
Michael Wyndham Thomas

Professor Challenger in Space
Quiet, the Tin Can Brains Are Hunting!
The Fear Man
His Nerves Extruded
The Doom That Came to Sea Base Delta
The Day the Moon Wept Blood
Stephen Theaker

Five Forgotten Stories
John Hall

Elephant
Harsh Grewal

Elsewhere
Steven Gilligan

November Spawned #1–4
Stephen Theaker (ed.)

New Words #1–4
John Greenwood, Steven Gilligan
and Stephen Theaker (eds)

Forthcoming Attractions

Thanks to Douglas for guest editing this issue!

Expect **Theaker's Quarterly Fiction #59** in March. We open to submissions for #60 on April 1.

You have until March 1 to vote in the **Theaker's Quarterly Awards!** See the blog for details.

Our blog is here:
www.theakersquarterly.blogspot.com

Stephen tweets every few days or so at:
www.twitter.com/Rolnikov

The zine has its own Twitter account too:
www.twitter.com/TheakersQrtly

Our email address is:
theakersquarterlyfiction@gmail.com

If you've enjoyed this issue, and especially if you haven't, please consider giving it a rating on Goodreads, or LibraryThing, or wherever you keep track of your books. Let us know you're out there!